CWYANE

(Kwayne)

A PETTY PRIVATE SCHOOL TALE

Anthony Edward DeFiore

As always, for my little girl

"Youth ages, immaturity is outgrown, ignorance can be educated, and drunkenness sobered, but **stupid lasts forever**." - Aristophanes

The cars lined up outside the farm sized school house. The Beemers and Mercedes stretched the acreage and roadway until they reached the busy street running through this burgeoning suburban sprawl. Escalades and Volvos littered the landscape but only for show. They were leases. Such is the life of the social and wealthy wannabes. It's polyester on the cheap. They live and die on secrets, manipulations and lies, and in the end, they resemble a sorority house instead of an educational academy.

The signage at this private school was of epic proportions. Stop, Go, No idling, Parking for 2.5 minutes only, This lane only, Turn only left after 8:03 am, Right lane ends, No soliciting, Avoid grass parking, Don't litter, New mother parking, Dr. John's Landscaping Surgery….. They sell private billboards on the school property to raise money for the school. This entire roadway was perhaps the length of one half of a city block. The need for control was offensive.

As the children prepared to leave from inside the building to play fun and games hopefully after school in some park or driveway, the true games were about to begin. They were games of astronomical importance for this ex-urb. The social climbing commences at the gym entrance. This is a true war of petty and frivolous social importance, indulgences and notoriety in a small hillbilly town. The battle of the aristocracy ensued on a suburban landfill.

When the school children began to disembark at the end of the day, one could see their faces fill with despair. It was a daily occurrence. Pilates with Mom, Stay safe at archery class, Hug and Jog with Mom runs, and as the mothers voiced their afternoon activities in a vain pursuit of status amongst the pseudo-bourgeoisie parent social climbers, the children's faces belied the true meaning of it all. It sucked. Mom's a control freak. Can't I just go home and play with her in the back yard. Can't I just play with my phone? Why is it always like this? Poor kids. Their parents think they're rich, but they are only plastic. Or maybe they just put it all on plastic and then disappear from Cwyane when the credit runs out… It has always been like this…

The plastic people are a creation of "*The Graduate*" Era. Remember the movie when the old guy tells the freshly minted college graduate Dustin Hoffman to go into "plastics"? Little did we know then, but the plastic people would be the fake people in that movie jump ahead to 2000. Plastic people. Plastic smiles. Plastic hair. Plastic personalities. *Stepford Wives* circa 1970. I blame the Television. In the 1960's and 1970's everybody wanted to be unique. Heck, most people barely had color TV back then. Everyone wanted to be who they are! Individuality. Now every over 40 something, who were children back then, want to be something else. They want to be like everybody else. It is quite sad. The same outfits, hair, personalities ~ it's *The Man in the Gray Flannel Suit all* over again in this Generation of Empowered Fools. It's really insecurity personified. In the end they all have colored hair, a "life is good" shirt and a hat with no team on it…driving a Hummer. It's like Woodstock went Lawrence Welk in a Sherman Tank. The fake people have fallen in step. The head master counted on that…

So who sends their children to private schools? The petty narcissists do. Double that. The Sociopaths do. These are the people who think they are better than others because they think that they have money. Mind you, these people clip coupons, go to "white sales" and know how much a quart of milk costs. They are really middle class people with delusions of grandeur. It is sad and rather embarrassing to hear them brag about the petty indulgences they enjoy among a crowd of people who really do have money and class. Then they are scorned like the refuse of the pseudo rich.

At Cwyane, when the pseudo bourgeois get parading and strutting their K Mart and Wal Mart style, crazy things happen. The insanity has no greater example than these are the people who buy their children roles in the middle school play by donating money to the head master. This is Broadway to them. Too bad it's about three steps below small town civic theatre. Like Mayberry on Steroids. These are the socially "woodsy" crowd attempting to climb the social ladder on the backs of their children. It is absurd. But these emotionally and economically disturbed people don't realize that their little monsters will be a plague on them their entire lives. And in the end, they won't talk to them very much either ~ and you can bet your arse they won't let their kids around them!

The small pseudo school "mums" and dads make up this petty bourgeoisie who never matured beyond 12. Things like character, honesty, civility and any sort of ethics never entered their frontal lobe with any maturation. As sociopaths, they always had a knack for making money. All that takes is no conscience. With greenbacks in hand, now they believe they are destined for greatness…albeit…vicariously through their children. These are the stage moms, the gymnastics moms, the pro field hockey moms at work here (sorry, there is no such thing as pro field hockey ~ LOLOL.). And don't get me wrong, the Dads are even worse. These are also the megalomaniac doctors and lawyers cavorting with each other under the guise of a middle school. THEY ARE ENTITLED TO IT by some act of God. And don't forget. Among people with this condescending psychopathy lie the true culprits. Bigotry and Ignorance. A lethal brew from before Socrates. But, when you create a schooling environment that is predicated on money or the impression of it ~ via Fox News & "Belief Superiority Syndrome", you will get these nightmare parents, and their pathetic children.

The truth of it is that while these parents believe that "buying everything" for the children is strengthening them. In short, they are weakening them for life. Like over feeding pig. They are going to end up barbeque. They will be timid antelopes being eyed by tigers. They will fear people of color. They will fear their own selves. They will seclude themselves in cookie cutter houses in woodsy developments…and build walls and canals to protect them within. Unfortunately, these enclaves will more resemble cemeteries than neighborhoods. They will create protected bastions of schools. Educational City States ~ with gates and moats. They will be isolated in their playgrounds, beaches and their "clubs". Soon they will atrophy in emotional and spiritual growth. Then, they will set their eyes on each other and devour themselves. Isn't survival of the fittest just grand? Eventually, you become so "fit" and isolated that you become the prey of evolution. Enter the Social Contract. But not here for these Cwyane Parents. They want to devour each other first. On behalf of their children, that is. YIKES! And then one day, some kid of one of these pseudo rich ~ in denial as to why their kid is "nuts" ~ walks into a school building and we have Sandy Hook or Columbine.

These private schools like Cwyane are not the Catholic Schools or the other religious schools. While those schools are certainly private schools and have narcissists of their own, at their core, these schools have a purpose to worship God in their curriculum. Basically, you know what you're getting there. Many of these schools are very, very good. But what does draw people to the opposite? What brings them to the small, pseudo elite, and private "non-secular" schools? It is the same thing that draws them to country clubs. You think it is money. But in truth, it is their inferiority complexes. I'll explain.

The elite private schools in our country educate the true .005%. It's probably less than that. The Rockefeller, Harriman, Roosevelt Families send their children to these schools like Andover, Choate, etc. They are about keeping the social order. But these other "wannabe" private schools think they are of the same caliber. They ain't even close. The wannabes are doctors, lawyers, and other assorted nouveau riche sociopaths who believe that in their small town that making over $200,000 a year qualifies them for the elite status in American society. Little do they know that they are the clerks for the truly elite and wealthy. It is sad. They lease fancy cars, but Cinderella never gets to the "ball".

Now some families send their children to these lower level private schools in order to have smaller class sizes, individual attention and some personal autonomy in their children's education. HA! Good luck with that one! These folks are in the vast minority, and are rudely misinformed. Most of the parents who flood these "country club" schools are nothing more than malignant narcissists trying to climb the social ladder which only leads to the bottom of the clouds. The true glass ceiling in America.

When public schools fail in an area (which is usually the result of racism in an ethnically changing geography), these little, pseudo bourgeoisie, educational city states pop up. They may have been established in a time when public schooling was not an American staple in order to educate many people in our country in need of schooling. But as the public schools grew in the US, these private schools turned into a bastion of gold diggers and phony baloney. These people have basically embarrassed themselves as they "think" they know everything about everything in education. As all narcissists do, they think they know about everything. These folks, however, are determined to insulate themselves from the public schools, create a separatist educational colony, and "hover" over their children relentlessly as their children build up resentment that will explode forth in a new generation of young thinkers. That is what Socrates was shooting for in Ancient Greece. He wanted parents to spoil and repress their children. He knew they would explode in thoughts. Unfortunately, many of these current private school children will become arrogant narcissists like their parents and many of the others will become drones and followers to rules, regulations and conformity. Fox News angry but conforming to everything brainwashing their minds. The good thing about narcissists who gather together is that it is much like a treatable disease. Eventually they are isolated and end up alone, powerless to fight back and eradicated like Swine Flu ~ or like Machiavelli…

And under the auspices of Master L.E. Berry, the Cwyane School subjugates the teachers of the school into being verbally abused by students, chaos in the classroom, adolescence fights turning into hysterical rages, grade inflation and changes, rules of assignments being broken because of how much your parents "give" and these teachers being in a constant state of either depression or exasperation ~ unless they become a zealot for Master Berry. And the money flows in….

~

The battery of parents waiting for their children lined the front door like a gaggle of geese flying south. The V formation subtly defined these parents own desires for status. They formed in their own little V for victory in the pursuit of Vain glory. But the battle was not truly ready to ensue until the headmaster walked out the door. He was more than a head master. At least in his head, he thought he was. His true game was to "bait" people into cliques to create a so called status hierarchy motivated by money with him at the top. Really he was a Head Master, and a baiter too. Maybe I misspelled? A Master-Baiter?

~

Beginning with his rather effeminate saunter between fake smiles and bow ties, this man of faux power understood his means of ascent. Money baby. He was the Head Master. He would wade in to the bullshit and grow like a rose. Seduce the unknowing rabble into believing your farce. Their pennies to Krugerrands will fertilize your ascent. Then turn this private (and at one time unpretentious) school into an Evangelical School and save these mortals from themselves. The balding head Master-Baiter straightened his glittering tie and began his beautification into the sheep of fools. He would now orchestrate the battle for the hearts and minds of this horde bedecked in gold, silver and cubic zirconia tennis bracelets. This jewelry was mostly J.C. Penney counter fakes. But don't blame Christianity on this one. No not at all. This school will be to "evangelize" the great Head Master of Cwyane. He is the sociopath that your mother warned you about. You can love God or love mammon. Not both. The Headmaster at Cwyane was a whore to the dollar from the first day he stole it out of his dad's poor box in his church.

Some would not be noticed. The scorn and ridicule would be unnerving to some. They were bludgeoned with a scarlet letter to mark their inferiority at the school. Some would flee in disgrace as the skin color of the school gradually crystallized into a true lily white from its previous spectrum of families. The head Master-Baiter reveled in his white parents. He never knows how to talk to the others. And still others are on his enemies list ~ to be shunned. The malignant, egomaniacal narcissist is well known to us all. However, they never really know themselves at all.

~

In the corner of this phalanx, there stood a man of average dress and size. Hustling out of work to retrieve his child for a set custody visit. He loved these moments. His child's smile relieved the tension of his day and of his divorce. He would kiss her on the top of her head and she would smile broadly. "Let's get a slushy Daddy!" his daughter would chirp. Why not? He was a Disney Dad for the next few hours. But first, before the joy, he would have to endure the battle. The battle of the plastic people.

~

Tommy was his name. He was a Dad. He came to get his daughter from school, but you would really think he was in the seventh circle of Dante's Sorority House Hell. You see. Tommy was being shunned. But Tommy wanted it that way. He saw the sociopaths coming from a mile away. Tommy knew that if he let the rumor sneak out that he hated to "shunned", that's exactly the treatment he would get from the Cwyane Faithful! So he let the game play on. Sociopaths can be so easily led by their nose when they only see to the end of the noses on their narcissistic face. They are manipulated by everything they hate that has ever been done to them. Little do they realize that other people don't have the same hang-ups.

Tommy would slowly get out of his car betwixt with both joyous anticipation of seeing his daughter and unyielding despair of ignorance that stood in front of him. To find his daughter he would have to endure hammering ignorance. Endure the game of battle of the phony power elite. C. Wright Mills described them with contempt for their idiocy. The local clique militia. Tommy would have to encounter "Shun for Fun" as it is known in the nearby City of Cwyane inhabited by the "other people". At the Cwyane School, it was a rite of passage.

Tommy smiled at a parent that he had never seen before. She seemed new he thought. Maybe she could be the person to be friendly with at the school. As they caught eyes, Tommy's smile was greeted with what is known as the "pivot" and "spin". It was the classic, Cwyane turn of the back. Then, there was always that pretentious giggle. Then, a whispering comment would be made to the other parents standing with this new mom. Then, the other people would turn their discerning eye to Tommy. Always with contrived purpose to let him know that they were talking about him. Then faces of disdain began. The noses went into the air. And Walla. "Shun for Fun" in its classic form. Some of us graduated from high school; some of us did not. Tommy laughed with joy!

Such assholes he thought. His laugh completely befuddled the "Shun for Fun" crowd.

Then, the "pivot" and "the spin" began the status battle. The Master-Baiter looked on with an approving smile. Watch the Philip Seymour Hoffman movie, *The Master*, and see how the cult like messiah ends up as the head of a private school in England. Hoffman's character destroys the sociopathic drama that rages at private schools in the USA. Mix in the movie, *Waiting for Guffman*, and the only problem is, the people it intends to disgrace, never notice it.

While Tommy had weathered the first dance of the day, he was vulnerable because he tried to breach protocol at Cwyane. He laughed to himself. He tried to be friendly to a stranger. But that is not encouraged at Cwyane. Cwyane keeps to its strict hierarchy status code. They know who they are. Outsiders beware. But there is a hole in the middle of this Lifesaver. It's the little place were phony people drown. For neither God nor Newton will be mocked. One will reap what one sows, and for every action there is an opposite and equal reaction. For Tommy, it had happened to him a thousand times before at Cwyane. He laughed in that Errol Flynn manner, and lately enjoyed it immensely. Such is the case when you encounter the insecure Cwyane parents. Tommy fondly referred to it all as "High School for Geeks".

As the new stranger pulled the old "pivot and turn" on him, Tommy smiled to himself. Well, he said to himself, they got to another one before I could plea my case. No matter. Geeks are geeks. No matter what label they wear on their clothing, inside that clothing they know that they are still nothing inside. Now, don't think for a minute that that kid you went to school with who had a runny nose and a pocket protector is being ridiculed here. He isn't. He's probably running some huge engineering firm in New York City now. Replete with a smile and self-satisfaction of a great life and career. No, these Geeks of the "High School for Geeks" were sometimes the cool kids in high school ~ whatever that means? They are the Geeks today who are reaching back to recreate the immature past that they believe was what life was all about. The high school nonsense that they were a part of has now become their life's ambition to enjoy…at their child's ELEMENTARY SCHOOL no less! The personal growth for them stopped at 12th grade. Maybe 6th grade? Remember how you would say to your college roommate, "That's sooo High School." Well, these Geeks never got that email.

While some of the "High School for Geeks" went to college to mature, educate themselves in a profession and move on with their lives, deep inside they knew. They knew that they were just trying to fill that hole created back in high school or middle school. It is education and maturity gone amuck. It is arrested development living in the world of elementary school recess. Halloween Parades, spelling bees and chorus concerts are all nice endeavors and fun to say the least....for CHILDREN. But when that's all your adult brain can grasp on to, as you approach your forties and fifties, well, let's just say, I'm glad somebody else has the missile codes instead of these bozos. The tales of their ridiculous behavior are legend. Tommy remembered one narcissistic parent who became so incensed at the fact that her paper flowers were not placed near enough to the stage during the school play (so she would be praised for her brilliant talent of paper flower making) that she pulled her child from the school play in protest. It was her show. The Cwyane School Play be damned. YIKES.

~

Cwyane was indeed "High School for Geeks". The worthless following the even less. Some of us look back at high school with a smile of our younger and much more immature world with a knowing smile of laughs, nostalgia and understanding. Unfortunately, most of us never do that. Those that never left are still lingering in the high schools of their minds trying to gain that status and acceptance that they were denied in their teen years. Little do these people realize that the place they are trying to reach isn't Cwyane's inner fiefdom. Really, it is the depth of their selves that they are trying to find. It is where their scorned little children reside begging to leave high school once and for all. And all this happens in front of the Cwyane school entrance every day. So much drama stirred up for so little. Some call it "Mama Drama". It would be a hit TV show. Reality TV at its finest.

Now it has been written in The New York Times, The New Observer and the New Orleans Times-Picayune that this is nothing new. The private school elitist game has been going on for hundreds of years in this country. The people who believe that they are better than the rest send their degenerate DNA, black sheep, inbred, country club refuse to the most prominent private schools in the US to maintain the hierarchy of status that brought us those favorable concepts of slavery, Wall Street swindles and Neiman Marcus.

But Cwyane was supposed to be different. Well, maybe it was once. When Estelle Cwyane started this wonderful little one room school house in 1870, she had a dream. It was going to be a student-centered approach to teaching the best minds in the Cwyane area. Those minds of course were primarily Lily white, but Estelle Cwyane searched for diversification in her town. "If you were smart," she implored, "Then I'm color blind." A wonderful person, who saw the future and was well in front of her Civil War Reconstruction Era. Today, most American schools are student-centered. However, over the century, Cwyane had slipped into the jungle of corrupting money. Estelle Cwyane kept up the good fight for many decades, but by 1960, she passed quietly in her sleep. With thousands of photos of all her "kids" who sent her photos and letters throughout their years extolling the triumphs and tribulations of people who had found their inside self and transformed it into a grand addition to their world. They melted away the plastic people veneer by 17. The children saw the world through the eyes of

Jungian ideas and practical math. They too would become part of a bigger world. But that was then, and this was now.

By 1960s, The New Frontier and The Counter Culture changed America for decades to come. But Cwyane didn't need to change. They were the harbinger of free thought, student-centered education and self-actualization. But as the 80's led to the money drug days of the 90's and 2000's, Cwyane lost its way. With Home Schooling and religious, evangelical affiliated schools (not the Catholic schools), Cwyane got hijacked by the religious right. They came in and hoodwinked the Cwyane leaders into a farce. That farce was construed by their head master. Fondly referred to in the City of Cwyane as "The Service Master" because he could brainwash anyone into his doctrine of cultism. The Service Master is the Master-Baiter. He just had many monikers. He was in need of getting back into reality, but more important, he needed to get off his cloud. He wasn't God, but he sure thought he was. Such is the fall out of the charismatic Episcopalian preacher syndrome that begets a sociopath.

So, under the noses of the Cwyane leadership, this venomous character showed up frolicking like the pied piper and the rodents followed. But the cliff led to another right wing, authoritarian, 80's prep school filled with religious fanaticism and obedience. Kids weren't going to be encouraged to think and speak and find themselves at Cwyane anymore. No, they were going to be brow beaten into obedience to the head master-baiter's view of America through the dark lenses of a David Koresh from Waco and Newt Gingrich. Yes, Cwyane went Wacko.

It is done ever so subtly at times. First, the Master-Baiter gains control of the small scholarship monies available at the school. While the school is to use the monies to attract excellent students from low income backgrounds and to attract these students to Cwyane through their tremendous academic abilities, when controlled by the "baiter" it is used to help his friends. These friends are the ones that promote his agenda of "purity" and "citizenry" when in reality these code words mean "white kids" from his choice of the racially pure. To illustrate this racism, The Master-Baiter once remarked in close company, "I never saw white janitors before I came to Cwyane." There is a snitch everywhere. The craziest addition to Cwyane by The Master Baiter was something called the Cwyane School Morning Prayer. He called it a "school collect" whatever the hell that was. The worst part of the "collect" were these words in succession. It read, "…make us pure, wholesome, truthful, obedient and true…" For a moment one might think he or she was reading Mein Kampf. But in these subtle words rang out a dangerous bias that extols bigotry and exclusivity. This thing never works in a democratic society that will eventually evolve and swallow this cultish nonsense whole. It becomes nothing more than a great waste of time. Ask Penn State and that "grand experiment"…LOL!

The baiter inundates the Cwyane School with code words. Some of these words are "fellowship", "society" and "friendship". However, the words are more sinister in their origin for the baiter. It is meant to inculcate the "right" people and the "club" people, and it means one thing in America. Exclusion and Bigotry. Call it Race or Religion if you will, but don't forget the issue of money. Cwyane is the baiter's pallet for "Whites Only". As the school declines in diversity, the typical race stereotypes find their way into the hidden curriculum at Cwyane. Right wing foundations provide the monies, and the so called symposiums on culture become nothing more than a "food day" activity or a tribute to Duke Ellington to placate the renegades who had hoped to send their children to a truly diverse school instead of an insulated Klan. As the class sizes dwindle and become "lily white", the Cwyane reputation as an exclusive country club grows. The sociopaths find other like sociopaths, and other friendly narcissists follow suit. After the Master's third year, a metal gate was erected at every Cwyane entrance. Fort Apache in dollar denominations had begun!

The only question for the baiter is, "Did you ever hear of General Custer?" No city-state stands forever, and by insulating with a goal of "ethnic" homogeneity, one can only see how the ruins of history illustrate this doomed endeavor. But unfortunately, the children of Cwyane are heard saying things to each other in the cafeteria in disgust. One child said, "What if God is Black? Vomit!" Another child lamented, "I hate going to my mom's medical office in the City of Cwyane. I hate seeing all those dirty people in the center of town." Ah, racism dies hard especially at Cwyane. Money and Racism are proportional in their growth.

~

At Cwyane, the High School for Geeks, the children of the neglected would now help their parents regain their lost status and popularity by gaining a place in this private.......elementary school. Indeed, it was only elementary school. It was the social pinnacle of nothingness. It is a place for children to begin their education. It is a place where old blackboard erasers go to die. At Cwyane, it truly was the bastion for the nouveau riche geeks trying to spark their personal climb up the local social ladder. Aggrandizing themselves by vicariously living through their kid's life. Or better, to return to something that never was for them ~ secondary school. Basically, these societal dwarfs fell into a small amount of money which of course they believe makes them part of the wealthiest 1%. But the 1% that they think that they are a part of is really them being the 1% that is laughed at by the truly rich. Nobody gets into that club. That's a genetic tree. You are born into that. Cwyane is like a turnpike rest stop for them. The Cwyane Geeks are simply the janitors in that world. The new pseudo rich never get a place at that table. That level of rich are the people who have their limos and drivers take their kids to school. They are the people who only see grocery bags when their house full of servants bring them in the back door to the kitchen. They have no idea what a gallon of orange juice costs. Cwyane parents have "box top" drives to raise $100. What does that tell you?

~

As Tommy stood in his own private, country club of one outside the school, he could see the encampments grow around him. Like Buffalo chips on the Great Plains they morphed into even larger cow dumps. He called them the "Cwyane pies". Sorta like "terd blossoms" were cow dump attempts to flower into tulips. But really they end up as mushrooms. They were encampments of the plastic fake of the high and mighty. If only they knew that they were in the company of coupon clippers hiding their pseudo wealth from the wretched crowd. These people know how much a dozen of eggs costs. But they hide it with their LIVES!

One little grouping would form, then another around Tommy. Their backs turned to him in unison as if it were a Medieval Ball. As these little circles formed, like the little groupings of pox marks on the face of adolescents, the dance continued. And in reality, that is who they were. They were little zits gaining the wrong attention on the faces of every one of these zealots at the High School for Geeks. It was like dancing in gym class. Never as much fun as kick ball.

~

The encircled bastions of status began to form on schedule as the headmaster stood at the doorway to the gym to announce exiting from school. He began to have a radiance surround him. He began to glow. He was being surrounded by a gold aura. Of course, this was in his mind…..For the Master-Baiter of the Cwyane School was about to wade into his congregation both divided and soon to be conquered by a master of the gods. He felt like it was Sunday in his reverend father's Indiana evangelical church. Preparing for his after sermon walk around. He thought he was exiting a farm house of chicks to compliment the mother hens. No roosters here. He was the only welcomed Rhode Island Red about to plant his seed. No one else would take his position. He was a gaawwdddddd. This was his barn yard when every day he brought forth the Sun with his crow. He ignored Tommy like a bastard step child. It had been going on this way with Tommy for eight years. It is amazing how these geeks can commence on rumor and innuendo to the point of an ignorant stifling. But then again, this was a high brow manure patch. Tommy always wondered why the headmaster wore a suit, suspenders, and a matching bow tie only to wear his decades old duck shoes as he left the gym doorway to gather his flock. Then it dawned on him. The headmaster knew that he was truly wading into manure in some Freudian way. It was the bullshit that he nurtured. It was all two feet deep.

~

The clamor of fake laughs and smiles filled the air. Pretention littered the scene with sarcasm. The commencement of the school time dismissal filled the hearts of the faithful. Would he recognize them today? Would he make them feel special with his smile or touch of the shoulder? Or would he look on someone else more favorably than them? The jealousy and uncertainty of the moment was palpable. Which parent would be favored today by the headmaster? Tommy could hear the director yell roll um.

Each circle was getting its fill of petty Cwyane gossip as the headmaster orchestrated it in his travels between them. Like feed being thrown at the circles of mother hens plucking and cackling as they ate up the status gained by each lie. Each time, as Tommy came to see over the years of this feeding frenzy, the last smirk or head wag would always end with a disgusted look at him or some other poor bastard. Oh there were others who received those same disgusted looks over the years. But they fled as time went by at Cwyane. Tommy counted the many lost allies in his head. They couldn't handle the "shunning". But they still remained Tommy's friends. He'd get their information and stories to his attorney in good time. But now the Sunday Stroll needed to be fulfilled by the Headmaster in a daily event just short of the resurrection. For Tommy, he wasn't going anywhere. He was going to stay at Cwyane in spite of the geeks and their hatred for him. He saw the emperor. Tommy knew he had no clothes on.

~

Then came the much anticipated and daily final charade. The mother hens were almost giddy at this point. The Headmaster had built up an air of anticipation as he would delay dismissal for a few minutes and then he would appear at the school house door as every eye would turn to him with baited breath. Hitler did that kinda shit. Then he would delay just a few seconds more at the doorway.

Just to titillate the crowd of 40ish and sex deprived women. When he could sense their moisture building, he would thrust into the crowd. They were orgasmic.

The Headmaster with his feathers up in full strut would walk by Tommy with a dance. He would pivot his right foot, raise his nose into the air, arch and sling his back ever so slowly at Tommy, and then move onto his final circle step with a fake gesture, point and shuttle in a two-step with an interested demeanor to his favored parent standing next to Tommy and proceed with a final conversation of nothingness. It was a well-rehearsed sequence befitting a royal ball. "I wanted to tell you about our masquerade party at the school for parents this weekend." he bellowed to his favorite parishioner parent of the moment. "No children, just our community. No extended community either," he cackled with a knowing tone. Tommy thought to himself. What the fuck is an "extended community"? Did he mean the civilized world outside this barn house? Tommy again thought to himself, "I'd rather have diarrhea than attend that fest." He thought maybe these people might join a country club instead of ruining their kid's lives at their school. But, such is the case of the wannabe. They can't afford the country club dues. And even if they could, the adulation by this

Headmaster was more enthralling. It's the Cwyane Farmhouse Elementary School or bust for them. They fainted in their excitement as the rooster came forth.

As each and every parent hustled their children away filled with gossip and cheer, Tommy always noticed that nobody ever kissed their children hello. No hugs. No "How was your day, sweety?" Just off to Mom and me Pilates in a burst no less. He guessed they had gotten their monies worth from their crowd; no need to talk to their children. If they had nannies, that would be her job. But they couldn't afford nannies. And, as always is the case, the final shun was for Tommy. Tommy started to position himself at the end of the processional each day to see if things might change. They never did. The turn away heads registered their shunning of him. They swerved to the right and to the left like Tommy was a car driving the wrong way right towards each of them. Tommy just counted. And his cell phone camera videoed every day from the dashboard of his car ~ perfectly positioned to register all the arrogance and contempt.

~

But now came the fun part. It was the treat for his day. On cue, his daughter would run from the door. "Daddy. Daddy. Daddy!" she would scream. Then a voice from hellish control would bark out. "Gina. Stop running." It was the elementary school fitness director Tammy Roadway. Gina froze in fear. Tommy looked at the bull-like, un-athletic, Fitness Director, and he said come here kid! Gina began to smile with joy and run again, and leaped into her Dad's arms. No control freak, recess aide can stop the love of a daughter and her Dad.

"I love you Daddy." Gina belted out. Tommy would always say, "I love you too Champ." It happened every time like this. It was their own little Cwyane Tradition amongst the feeding hens. Tammy Ridgeway scowled. She was foiled again in her pursuit of controlling this obstinate male. She would emasculate him soon enough she pondered. She had tried to stop Tommy's and Gina's little tradition before, but to no avail. In fact, Tommy once received an anonymous letter that this running by his daughter might cause him to be brought before the board of the school trustees for a reprimand. Tommy laughed at the letter and said "Reprimand! Maybe I'll get detention! Fuck um." Tommy enjoyed this all with a joy only a father could know. It looked like Tommy won this skirmish on this UN-civil war like battle ground. Gina and Tommy skipped to their car in the parking lot. The head master scowled. "I will run him out of here eventually," he muttered under his breathe. Lex Luther was foiled by Super Dad again.

~

Tommy couldn't help himself. He said to Gina loud enough for the headmaster and the fitness director to hear, "They better be careful or someday, someone might drop a house on them too." Gina sardonically laughed, "Ohhhhh Daaaaad. That's the wicked witch." Tommy responded with a devious smile at the rabble, "I know kid, I know." Then they both laughed and off for a slushy they went with the war torn field littered with human debris and wounded egos. Not a place for the weak hearted.....or the mature for that matter.

~

It's called relational bullying. It's a preadolescent behavior that if not treated, it will turn into a plague for adults to inflict unto others. Sort of like a cult like congregation or a country club. The problem as it manifested itself at Cwyane was that it was being nurtured by the Un Fitness Director and the Headmaster. You see ~ they are country clubbers ~ or at least they think they are. The fees for the country clubs are probably too high for them so they tackle the next best thing. An elementary school. But the sadistic behavior is not only sick, but it really is treatable. It's called growing up. Most bullying stops at 13 or so. Kids get it. They go through a maturity spurt in their heads and their souls, and it's done with. But for wackos, the disease lurks well past middle age. And when used as a tool for power and control, it can create a cult.

Relational bullying works like this at Cwyane. The Master-Baiter selects from his list of qualified applicants ~ the wannabes of a small circle of town ~ and he grooms them into his inner circle of cadres destined for elementary school immortality. Hitler created the SS from just the same type of group of sycophants who were so delusional of their own greatness they thought they could kill almost every Catholic, gypsy, Pole, Russian and Jew in the world. It's a lovely experiment of creating an "elite" small group who are flushed with compliments and public praise to the point that they believe their own press clippings. In reality, they are being brainwashed into a "society" or more like flushed down a commode. The horrible part at Cwyane is that as the young elementary school kids watch their parents shun, turn their backs on people and rumor monger, they pick up the nasty bigoted habits. Shit begets shit. Apple doesn't fall too far from the tree. You know. So as their parents do it, so do the kids. They pick out the weakest of the group or the most talented but nice kid in their grade, and they proceed to gang up on them in bully style. "Boys will be boys" and "girl world" are phrases used by the idiot parents and pseudo professionals who let relational bullying thrive instead of using the "teachable moment" to help children become good people, citizens or whatever they want to be. Instead, the kids become SS qualifiers. The kids who get bullied ~ well let's just say that in the extreme there weren't too many serial killers who weren't ostracized by their peers at a young age. In the middle of the bell curve, bullying destroys people from the inside out from an early age. Then they grow up to be Head Masters...

Gina took a dose of relational bullying at Cwyane when a girl who was jealous of Gina's friendliness and talents took it upon herself to inform her friends that if they spoke to Gina, she would shun them into oblivion. These young and innocent girls wanting friendship at 12 years old figured: well Gina is always nice to me, so I'll shun her to gain so and so's friendship as well. The shunning extending to the parents as some of the girls began to be rude to Gina's mother as well. Could this all be a planned attack by narcissistic parents attempting to impose their will on other adults by using their children as pawns at Cwyane? You bet your ass it was.

The assault usually begins with a typical elementary school slight. It starts with somebody not liking your favorite sports team or somebody not telling you that your pencil case is pretty. In any event, it festers until it becomes rage and a mania. It could take a few months or a few years. It could take a blink of an eye. Couple this with very small incestuous classrooms where Cwyane students rarely get away from each other and mix in the cult techniques of a power hungry Head Master, and there you have it. The Waffen SS.

Using children to further one's own gain is as common and pathetic in our lives as the fifty percent divorce rate and child custody battles. But with the snitty, country club mentality of Cwyane, it borders on sociopathic. But then again, only a sociopath would ever strive for the inner circle of power found at a private elementary school. Much like wanting all the toys in a sandbox to be on your side ~ we outgrow it because we are taught to share and to be nice to people. At Cwyane, with all the phony ethics / virtues training of the Master-Baiter and "inculcating" (the word is actually used in Cwyane brochures to sell the positive attributes of the school ~ like people want their kids to be brainwashed), children find themselves being picked off the chessboard of school life by the harrowing escapades of adults viciously striving for their own narcissistic medal of honor. It's worse than Kafka could write.

So Gina got saddled with relational bullying for about two months. She and her Dad monitored it while Gina's mother ignored it. Ignoring it just feeds bullying. It's like putting Miracle Gro on a dandelion patch. After Gina couldn't take it anymore, her Dad decided to talk to the parents of the girl bullying Gina. Lo and behold, the parents were very responsive. They knew right from wrong....for a short time anyhow. After talking with both girls about being friendly to each other, the problem went away. Being nice does that. But the Master Berry SS got wind of this harmony, and they would have none of it. Gina's Dad was not in the country club. Gina's Dad was not in the "group". How DARE he try to solve an easy problem like this between parents! Doesn't he know that all answers come from Master Berry and FD Roadway? Yes, and a bidet is a drinking fountain.

The Cwyane Brown Shirts began to inflict such a torrent of rude and uncivilized behavior towards Tommy that it resembled a pack of wolves. Rumors about Tommy flew through the school grades. The rumor mill in a small bigoted and ignorant community swirls like lightening, and it borders on the absolute ridiculously insane! "Did you know that he molested a child" said one sick parent (unfortunately this parent had been molested; became a sociopath; and spent the rest of her life accusing everyone besides her father who had been the abuser). But, she was BELIEVED at Cwyane. Bizarre! Worse yet, one parent who had just watched Law & Order SVU was convinced that another parent wearing a trench coat at the school play was really concealing an AK47 ready to blast the entire Cwyane Community onto the lead story on MSNBC, CNN and Faux News! The imaginary becomes reality when a group of gaggling women and twerpy men get together in small numbers. The best thing about the "TV Drama" turned real is how idiotic the gossiping country club set looks when their rumor turns into complete bull shit! LOL! Tommy would tease them relentlessly. He would send the most crazed Cwyane Parents coupons in the mail for "Gun Shows" and "1/2 Price Assault Weapon sales" at the local sporting goods store. These wild eyed and insane Cwyaniacs would send messages through the Cwyane Rumor Mill like a torrent storm! Tommy couldn't help himself. He would laugh uncontrollably when he would get petrified looks from the Cwyane Country Club set.

The "turn" and the "twirl" were being used like it was a tilt a whirl ride at a fair. Tommy could actually feel a breeze at times as these weight watching cougars spun their web of "shun for fun". But the worst of it was the physical slights to Tommy. Tommy found himself being ignored to such a point that parents would rudely cross right in front of him (within an inch or two) just to get where they wanted to go with no excuse me or pardon me. The worst was when their children began to see Tommy as a tackling dummy or misplaced chair. Their children would bump into him mercilessly whenever they saw him standing by himself at a school event. Lord knows he couldn't draw a crowd. Then the real terror hit.

One set of parents attempting to fulfill the Master-Baiter's desire and dictum to "rid me from this burden" actually sent their child to bump into Tommy, fall down, and then start to cry and blame Tommy for hitting him. This horrid manipulation was put into action with three specially designed witnesses to see the entire event. They were positioned at three of the four corners of the gym anteroom. As the child lay forlorn and crying, a crowd of SS members descended on the scene. All of a sudden Master-Baiter appeared on cue. Tommy thought he was dead. How could he combat this diabolic scheme? As a bigger crowd formed around the assault, some parents said, "He did it because he's a Muslim." "Yea." said another, "He's not Cwyane." Tommy swore he saw Joe McCarthy wink at him from behind a classroom doorway. As the mania continued and the voices of anger cackled from the mob, a funny thing happened. It happens like this from time to time. It is as if God reaches down from Heaven to solve a mundane human travesty. From out of the corner of the hallway, Gina's previous adversary ~ the bully who started the whole mess to begin with ~ lurched forward. In a blink of an eye an angelic glow came over her and she yelled, "Stop." You could have heard a pin drop. The mob of adults went hush. The scene became quiet. The little girl spoke. She said, "I saw the whole thing. Gina's Dad didn't do anything." The mob stayed silent. The moment was frozen. And as if by divine intervention, the entire fiasco ended. The hysteria subsided. The mob coward off into anonymity. The little boy who was crying bloody murder jumped up and ran away. Tommy thought he was at the movies. It ended. As the aftermath transitioned into people twirling and spinning, Master-Baiter had captured the entire event on his phone camera. Tommy addressed him, “Would you please forward that video to me on my cell phone?” The Master-Baiter scowled at Tommy, and then he smirked as he showed Tommy his phone and hit his delete button. He twirled and fled. But as the scene became a memory, a third grader came up to Tommy. He stammered out, “Mr. Tommy, I can send you the video on my phone.” Tommy smiled. From children the truth and justice came forth. A third grader with an iPhone.

But isn’t it always like that…

~

The Cwyane Country Farm School. For a moment in the late 1990’s, Ethel and Joseph Cwyane tried to re-establish their mother’s school under the goals she brought forth in the 1880’s. This academic institution with great hopes albeit a small classroom was what made Cwyane. It was a one room school house with a big barn next door in which they created a place to learn / to enrich the lives of their children and their friends in the classic learning style. No Mom Pilates here.

Say what you want. The old way in education works, and it fosters the desire to "learn for life" creating numerous professionals, community leaders and scientists in the local community. Today, the local community of Cwyane is an afterthought to the "community" of Cwyane. The City of Cwyane is a place to be feared as the plethora of darkened faces has grown over the years. Although these faces are darker, they still boast of the same educated professionals and scientists that Cwyane believes can only come from their "white" front door.

Sorry to say, most of the girls at Cwyane grow up to be soccer moms only with no real jobs and the boys become middle management waiting for their parents or boss to give them approval. It is a sad measure of a school that never seems to create much but a social hierarchy amongst themselves. Tommy had researched other private schools for Gina. He was happy to see that when the word "community" is used on the other school websites, it usually refers to the surrounding city or town.

It was truly a shame that the Cwyane kids could not recapture the glory of their mother's school. They quickly pulled their children out of the school. No more Cwyane(s) at the school of their family name. Cwyane was now a city-state. The only thing missing was the moat.

~

The disturbing part about the Cwyane "community" is that it seems to employ the identical attributes found in cults. Secrets, Lies and Manipulations. Everything is attempted to be handled in house. Brush it under the "community rug". Solve the dilemmas amongst the "community". Keep the secrets in the "community". Only deal with our own "community". And it is done with the most false and plastic faces of administrators and brainwashed parents. It sometimes is truly horrible. During the last year, there was a mysterious death at the school. A parent was killed in a brutal attack by the daughter of another family. It was done with a lacrosse stick. When the police arrived, the headmaster wouldn't allow them onto the premises. In moments, a report came to the police that the woman was dropped off at the local hospital. No one knew who drove her there. The headmaster gleefully told police with a smile of plastic deceit, "See. Nothing happened here." The noticeable smell of Clorox and other chemicals wafted through the second grade classroom where the assault was supposed to have taken place. As police arrived with search warrants in the morning, nothing could be found. Every morsel of evidence seemed to disappear, and a classroom full of students, ten parents and two teachers saw absolutely nothing. Jim Jones was smiling somewhere.

~

Let me give you the description of the Cwyane Parent. It is the mother. The father could be a dildo for all it matters to the women at Cwyane. It is the type of matriarchal nightmare that fosters a man hate that can only be described as the Women of the Amazon hunting men for sport. To castrate them is the goal, and a bottle of formaldehyde sits on the mantle of every control freak woman at Cwyane, and it contains a pair of their husband's balls. There is basically a prototype dad at Cwyane too. He is a twerp cowering in the shadow of his wife usually a professional (doctor or lawyer); to be seen and not heard. This dad can also serve as the school gadfly making paper mache animals for a school event or managing the teacher gift fund at the end of the year. In any way, he is the tool of his mom…I mean his wife….

The next kind of dad is the Type A Narcissist/Sociopath. He is in vain pursuit of glory in his chosen profession and then out sailing the Caribbean in a competitive yacht race or bagging Elk in Wyoming ~ usually without his family. Raising the kids is his wife's job. He is just the narcissist dad who considers his children as objects for him to point to at executive lunches when describing "his" exploits of being the perfect father. He wonders why after they leave the nest for college that he never hears from them. At Cwyane, kids flee to boarding school after 8th grade.

Let it be said to the dads of this ilk. If you don't peel the potatoes, you don't get gravy on your mash potatoes at the Thanksgiving meal. And you usually don't get a house full either. The next dad is the slave driver type "A" narcissist who is determined to get his son or daughter into the professional league of his, the dad's, choice. The kid is an athletic drone or a musician punished into pursuing an art that he will grow to hate because of the relentless "bleacher dad" who drives him like a mule. That's about it on the dad front. The men who don't fit the bill find themselves home by five for dinner and confronting an empty house while his wife and kids are out at some Cwyane "how to buy luxury furniture" presentation, or Cwyane "how to raise your male child" seminar, or how to decorate your home for the Cwyane Christmas gala tour. That is the tour of "Cwyane Parent Homes" at Christmas time. The Cwyaniacs hop on a motor coach bus and go and genuflect in front of the holiday décor of other Cwyane Parents. What confused Tommy was that a former Cwyane Parent who fled the school would decorate his home around Christmas with such grandeur that the local newspaper would feature the lights and decorations in its Local Section. People would drive by the house and be filled with Christmas Cheer. Neighbors would come by and carol beautiful songs almost every night. But the guy could never get on the Cwyane House Tour? "What's wrong?" he asked, "My lights aren't good enough for you?" Well my friend, at Cwyane, you see….. ALL your decorations must be approved by the Decoration Committee. Your decorations must be of a certain value, and they must be INSIDE your home. Tommy got it even if his buddy didn't. You were "permitted" to display a string of lights around a window, but the committee frowned on "blow ups" etc. There was even a hierarchy drawn regarding the Holiday House Excursion. Cliques and committees. All designed with the Grinch in mind. With all this anarchy of affluence, Cwyane was pigeon holing the existence of so many, many Dads as they sank into a lonely existence as the "Community of Cwyane" swallowed their family whole. Quite abnormal in an America in which a Dad dedicated to his family might be usually playing catch with his son in the front yard or at a tea party for his five year old daughter on the living room floor. Just regular America doing regular things. Of course, that ain't Cwyane. Cwyane is for the "better" Americans. We'll "inculcate" our values into your children so the recruitment slogan is written onto their advertising signs on the few lawns of the wayward souls in the City of Cwyane.

The unfortunate family behavior at Cwyane seems to be stratified into a few separate types. It becomes the preoccupation with preoccupations. The narcissistic desire to be immortal or even greater than God … because they think they have mammon. The sad truth about small private schools is that it caters and attracts those sociopathic parents who consider themselves rich when they really aren't, they consider themselves the "elite" of us all when they really aren't, and they have kids who they think are better than any kind on the earth….when they really aren't. And they all fine dine at "The Tilted Kilt". :o

As Tommy and Gina followed the "elite" into school one early am, one such obsessed parent leaned over to her sociopathic child in training, and watched admirably as the sociopathic child ignored the African American Catholic Priest leaving the school after dropping off admission pamphlets at Cwyane. The pamphlets were for any interested students for the local Catholic Jesuit School. At Cwyane, those pamphlets immediately found their way into the waste can. The Roman Catholic Priest was filled with a horrid shock on his face as the child made a derisive scowl at him. His mother patted him on the head and said, "That's good Ethan, you don't have to be nice to them; they aren't equal to us." Oh my, Saint Peter!

What is even worse (if it were possible!) is that these sociopathic parents are the ones who professionalize their children at a young age. They want that scholarship in a sport for their kid or they want to watch them on television at the Olympics. Too bad that they never televise Olympic Field Hockey or most women's sports…Regardless of the fact that their kid might just be above average, but not Usain Bolt or Michael Johnson. No, these are the ever scheming wannabe parents, who have children who lack the God given talent. These are the children who have their entire existence cannibalized by their vicariously living parents who want the golden medal….for themselves mind you. In a large school, there is room for all types of people and children. Just like the USA. People will naturally group with like people. But they won't exclude the people around them who are unique in other ways. They form their own friendship groups. And the best part is that the sociopaths and narcissists are ALWAYS attracted to like personalities in the hope of gaining status, but they all end up looking at empty mirrors like vampires. Isn't it fitting that sociopaths, narcissists and vampires always suck the blood of emotions out of the caring people only to be exposed and destroyed either by each other or sunlight! It is the nature of their failing sojourn in life.

The problem at a small school littered with the sociopathic is that it ostracizes the granite-like different people in the hopes of molding the malleable into cultish zealots dominated by television ads. The term "hurried woman syndrome" is born of neurotic woman and men who spend every waking hour finding lint on their jackets and driving their kids into OCD problems at a small private academy. And these geeks find obscure sports for their kids to play like squash, fencing and archery. Another obscure part of Americana…

In a larger school, the natural forming of groupings of parents and children helps to add diversity to a school and augments its talents instead of streamlining them into a cult. Why does it happen? To this end, we've all seen those fake and plastic smiles and laughs on television ads all our lives. Those who can discern the bull shit out don't have time for the cliques of face formers that herd at a small school like Cwyane. They don't have time to create ever shrinking circles of elitist fraud in some vain attempt at glory ~ vicarious that is, through their kids. The nausea that this creates in the truly better selves of our planet also finds these better selves avoiding the nonsense of a Cwyane School. If only these people were concerned more about the education in the classrooms of Cwyane, and not the exclusive parking spots and social pecking order of pseudo elites. If only the blind could see at Cwyane. They might look into a mirror and really see nothing.

The mother and dad from the above descriptions are representative of a certain kind. The first is the parents consumed with the professionalism of a two year old. Cwyane is littered with the professional gymnasts, ballet dancers, child “TV Stars”, youth astronauts, squash player or the next American Idol. There are stage mothers galore! Acting lessons, voice lesson, photo shoots, lessons on their lessons until the unknowing become the “unwillings” and the bitter child becomes an unfulfilled adult who thinks they let their parent down or grandparent ;) These are the parents and grandparents of the unfulfilled dream. The one that lives through the youth of others ranting and raving on the sidelines of each game or mouthing every word from the front row of every play or musical that their child has a line. It is the sad culmination of a life lost to status that has ruined an adult and eventually ruins a child. 18,000 to one. Those are the odds of a child being raised into a professional of sport. For acting it’s even higher. Dreams of TV stardom and millions for parents that lead a kid down a road of ruin until they get a second chance. When they ruin their kid’s life in the OCD pursuit of vain glory. Remember parents who just played “who can spot the next red car” on a trip to the ice cream shop with their kid? Not these avaricious deludes. These parents scold their kids not to ask for "sprinkles" on their ice cream cones because they "might get fat!" Sad people make even sadder kids.

~

Cwyane has many traditions. In a school full of 40 something mothers desperately pushing their fat into spandex outfits entirely too small and young for them to wear, the school mascot is a cougar. How fitting. How laughable. But the closest young buck that these cougars are ever going to snare are the bucks found in their husband's wallets. Sorry Mrs. Robinson. You are as desirable as a pimple on a fly's ass. Or better yet, you aren't desirable anymore no matter how many Avon products you transfer to pretty jars and containers bought on line. Just know that your husband's buy those pretty blue boxes and ribbons on line too ~ and pass off the fake jewelry to you as Tiffany. Sad to say, these cougars wouldn't know Tiffany from Salt Water Taffy. The pretentious know-nothings know nothing. Hey let's have a tea party.

~

Gina and her Dad were having a blast after school. The slushy sugared them up, and they ran thru the immense park and playground without a care. They played on every jungle gym, park toy and swing. The Bliss of a sunny day. But then it happened. They saw a small group of people having a snack at the picnic tables just beyond their view. Tommy said, "Hey kid, let's say hello. Maybe you can play with these kids while Dad rests his back for this late 40's guy." "Ohhhhh Dadddddd!" Gina said. Then she said, "Let's race." And she took off. Tommy took off with her and they laughed and huffed and of course Gina beat her Dad in a close race. Tommy figures that he has lost every race, hop scotch, checkers game and Wii game for four years, so, why not lose one more?! His record is 0-4,325. A Good Dad always lets the kid win.

As they approached the tables, laughing and huffing, Gina froze. The glorious smile disappeared from her face as her eyes caught the sight of the table's occupants. The eyes from the table knew and adored Gina, but they did not care for her dad. From the eyes of many years to the eyes of just a few, the complex structure of relational bullying ensued. The goal was of course to drive Gina into that forlorn Catch 22 of adoring her dad but wanting to be accepted by others ~ that was the "Cwyane Posse". As if by design, the group unceremoniously and instantly gathered their belongings and fled. Gina was motionless in her fear of wanting to love her dad and have her friends approval ~ and their mom's approval too. As they fled, they looked over their shoulders with a snarl. Tommy noticed one of the parents. Gina knew who they were well before her dad. She saw her friends. She saw a CWYANE sweat shirt. She was hurting inside. This nonsense happened all the time. As the group loaded into their cars, Tommy yelled, "Hey, you lost a diamond tennis bracelet here." Gina said, "There's no bracelet here Dad." Tommy said, "I know honey but they will be pooping in their pants if they think they will have to slime back here to get it while we are here." Gina smirked, but then she frowned. It was always so hard on her. Too bad that the parents who orchestrated this nightmare didn't understand how much it hurt her or even gave a shit! "Don't worry Gina, we're going," Tommy said, "We'll leave it right here for you." Tommy yelled at the Cwyaniacs.

As Gina grimaced with fear that the parents might know it was a lie, and tell Gina's mom, she also thought it might be fun to play with her dad! She loved playing with him no matter, as Gina put it, "Dumb and Un Fun those other parents are…including my mom!" Then Tommy said, "Gina, let's go hide over there for a minute." So they went into a thatched little grove about ten feet away. "Why are we going her Dad?" said Gina with trepidation but also a fun little smile. "Wait, this should be fun." said her Dad.

As Gina and her Dad hid, one of the mother's slowly sulked towards the invisible bracelet on the picnic table. She was flustered…again. She carried a 5 inch tree stick with her. "To ward off a rapist like me," Tommy chuckled to himself. Murmuring again to herself how she could be so stupid to forget the bracelet. As she arrived at the table, she looked and looked and looked, but couldn't see anything. Where was it? She threw her arms up to her fellow Cwyane Cult Cohorts and was again beguiled by the whims of life. Then Tommy said to Gina, "Watch this."

In a low, gravel-like voice, Tommy began to growl and rustle the sticks and leaves around them. Then it got a little louder and menacing. The Cwyaniac Mom was bedeviled with instantaneous fear! She was frozen in her stance! She was petrified!

Now a normal human would have fled. But this is an over-burdened, not very bright control freak who has been made to feel anxiety like a professional from her daytime TV dramas. She seemed to be lost and afraid all at once. Was it a West Nile Virus

Beast come alive, Killer Bees, an Avian Flu bird, or a Swine attacking with Flu?! The woman was beside herself. Then as the hand of panic touched her on the shoulder, she ran back to the cars in a wobbling sprint befitting a Rhino in heat. “It was a wolf I tell you. A WWWOLF.” she screamed as the Volvos and Lexus wagons turned up dust and screeched away out of the parking lot in terror with sippy cups and juice boxes bouncing on the roadway and blowing in the wind!

Gina and Tommy fell on the ground in hysterics! They were beside themselves in laughter. Joyous laughter. Gina yelled at her Dad, “Mom’s gonna find out Dad. She’s gonna be mad.” Tommy looked at her with a tear in his eye, “Not you sweetheart. I’m gonna be the one. And don’t you just love it??!” Finally, Gina broke free of the monster in the closet who tormented her every day and with every Cwyane related movement and action, and she smiled as brightly as the sun! “That’s my little girl!” her Dad yelled. Gina said, “Dad, are you gonna pee? Well are you? You always say that you’re gonna pee when you laugh hard.” Tommy exclaimed back, “Noooooooo, Noooo, sweetheart. I just say that, but I’ll tell you; today, I was darn close!” They laughed hysterically again as the evening shadows descended onto the playground. Gina blurted out in relief of many different shades, "OHHHH DAAAD." And they laughed all the way home.

~

A little bit about the reputation of Cwyane. It wasn't always like this. Before the recent evangelical crusade of sociopaths initiated at Cwyane, the school was known as a rigorous academic school with a tradition of community involvement (In the city of Cwyane). Programs designed to augment student awareness of culture, a world view and a commitment to the surrounding neighborhood city or community. Cwyane participated in local City of Cwyane Halloween Parades, spaghetti dinners at the VFW and The Cwyane School helped to run the soup kitchen. The Cwyane kids were involved in the city and the children and the school prospered for it.

However, once the huge inward focus began at Cwyane via Master Berry, the local involvement ceased. Narcissus looked into the Cwyane City Pool and he saw darker faces than his own. There was no love lost. "Oh My God!" they could be Catholics too!" he roared in disapproval! And in short order, you could see the multicultural enrollment dwindle away at Cwyane as the students from Belize, India, Mozambique, Russia, China and Guatemala changed to a more Protestant Euro-centric and "white" student body. And these kids weren't white kids from the City of Cwyane. Within this "new" white student body a push towards a WASP and pseudo WASP culture seemed to emerge. Ids, I mean, Kids began to appear from out of nowhere in Beemers and Botox with wallets filled with ever increasing tuition dollars. Gone were the days of Chinese New Year Celebration, Brazilian Festival and Black History Month. Enter Figgy Pudding and fish & chip lunches. The school's radical shift away from a world view and a more "Un-Catholic" point of view was giving way to a Protestant evangelical view of the world. And to think this all happened as Barak Obama became President of The United States. The new pronunciation of Cwyane (K-Wayne) School amongst the City of Cwyane Citizens now became SWINE. As the wagons circled even more at the Cwyane School, one can only recall the phrase, "Hogs get fed; Pigs get slaughtered." World culture dimmed at the Cwyane School. The massacre ensued.

~

For Tommy Stugats (Yes, he's Italian), the carnage began as soon as he got divorced from Gina's Mom. With a large gaggle of man haters at her beckon call and a "poor me" attitude, Gina's Mom initiated a war zone for Tommy at Cwyane. Also, a burgeoning group of twerps began to form at Cwyane to help in the banishment of Tommy. While it is not a big deal to hang out with your kinda folks, it is when the goal is destroy someone in a small town.

As it is the case in any petty sorority house, the truth was the first casualty. Rumors began to fly in the school about Tommy being a pedophile, a wife beater and a chiseling divorce opponent. "And did you hear, he's in the Mafia…" whispered The Master of them all. He knew when he could fan a flame to raise money. Watch the Sopranos, Give me more money and I'll run out this cur!

The most unfortunate rumor regarding Tommy was the most horrific. And, with Tommy being devoted to his wife and a strong Catholic, it didn't help him in the least with the devoted atheist who spread this rumor. It seems that one's hate for God finds many avenues for adventure in life. It is especially interesting for a hateful man hater who took up the sword for Tommy's ex-wife to defend her and destroy Tommy's reputation. This under-sexed, over wrought, bi-polar misandrist was determined to put Tommy's scalp on her mantle.

It would soon be "The Big Lie" at Cwyane, and Tommy Stugats was the target. After growing to hate her mother over the decades and the loathing of her sexually abusive, alcoholic Dad, and after, emasculating her live-in unmarried "husband", Lilith Doglinski needed a new challenge in her life. She was set to initiate her new escapade and to rumor monger Tommy into oblivion at her cherished Cwyane. Oh, and she had help. It seems that these sociopath / borderline types draw a crowd made up of sycophants and other psychopaths catering to their every whim and fancy. They are mostly similar woman and men with the dogged edge to kill other men for the same reasons as Lilith. If you see only one thing about Cwyane, please recognize that the emotionally disturbed flock to private schools like Cwyane in droves.

The initial reason people send their kids to Cwyane is to receive the best education for their children that money can buy. But the problem starts after that. Of course, they have the "money" to send their children to a "rich kids" school. People who have a great deal of money that they earned, as apart from inherited, have a blood thirsty lust to make more and to have the best for themselves. And somewhere along the way, they have stepped on the throat of some very close friend, colleague or sibling to get to their financial promised land. And it doesn't even break their stride to do it or to feel anything. Because they can't feel any emotions. As for their children, they are merely extensions of their arms. Pawns on the narcissist's chess board of life. Their children have no identity except for what they can do for the sociopath. It is vicarious living on the backs on the truly weak ~ abused children. These people are the sociopaths of America bedecked in the jewels and the power of pseudo wealth intimidation that purchases lesser people of ethics all in the name of avarice. Interestingly enough, these sociopaths need mirrors for themselves. So they look to find others like themselves in order to keep up appearances. And eventually, they find a school like Cwyane. It's all pretention with smoke and mirrors. It starts with a chance meeting at a hospital lunchroom or elevator in City Hall. The sociopaths begin to filter out the "less than" others until they come upon their identical narcissistic twin. And many times these people look exactly like each other. And they sit and gaze into each other's eyes with a blank adoration. They become spell bound with the reflection of another narcissist in front of them. And in short order, all their children are going to Cwyane! And the student body at Cwyane grows exponentially, as sociopaths find social and educational bliss. But, unless someone says that the Emperor has no clothes on…nothing changes for the better. But first, the Master Baiter must fill Cwyane with a majority of these wackos. It is easy when he worships money. They "pay to play".

As for the people who just wanted the best education for their kids, close attention, small class sizes, etc. Well they got fooled. So long Charlie, you joined a country club. Education is second to money here at Cwyane. As the disappointed families sulk out of Cwyane without financial aid with the shame for wanting a good academic school, The Master fills their slots with the friends of the sociopaths. Sort of like the Friends of Freud instead of Bill W. These are the sociopathic doctors, lawyers, stage mothers, business executives and borderlines who gaggle and grouse together brought into cultish unison by the emotional debacles of their childhoods that has scarred them into the emotional decay of every narcissistic monster. And it gets worse from here. The snitty, condescending and country club attitude comes with them. Sprinkle in a little Fox News and you have a genuine sociopath with "Belief Superiority Syndrome". That's where you have your beliefs political or otherwise, and because you have it repeatedly drummed into your head every day on TV, you choose to develop an Air of Superiority of your beliefs and you condescend abusively onto the rest of us "Non-believers"…Mitt's 47%... LOL! And these political werewolves have friends. And in this age of keeping up with the "Jones" and the tea party, borderlines of a feather flock together. And when they get together….well Tommy Stugats….look out!

As Tommy's ex cried to Lilith (Lil) her woes, she continued to have an affair with the assistant headmaster. Little did Tommy's ex realize it then, but she was going to be the janitor for the Cwyane Sociopaths for as long as she didn't realize it. Unlike "Frick and Frack", Tommy's ex was paying for it one way or another. So after a two year fling, Tommy's ex was convinced by Lil and the other man hating Cwyaniacs that a divorce from Tommy was in order, and they would run Tommy out of the school for her to make it easier on her divorce transition. Tommy was that bastard, wife beating, wise guy pedophile that he wasn't. But the truth was the true orphan here. Not Lilith's poor abused adopted daughter.

With Lilith by her side….and I mean ALWAYS by her side…the attack began as a whisper. They are replete with dirty scowls and condescending glares. Then it spreads into a full-fledged rumor. Then it became slander. Lil had an axe to grind against Tommy beyond her general hate for men and her child raping Dad. She fully believed that Tommy had called child protection services on her to register a child abuse claim. Even though, Lil had gone through sixteen nannies, au pairs and babysitters in three years of service for reasons never discussed in the hallways of Cwyane. Lil was convinced Tommy had made the call. I believe it is called a disassociation fixation. To help with this war on Tommy, Lilith recruited another cohort. Betty Flinch. Elizabeth Flinch was a poor, shanty Irish bastard whose mother was an alcoholic and her Dad abandoned the family at Betty's birth. Betty Broderick had a clone. It was Betty Flinch. But Betty had a husband. Emerald Flinch. "Em" Flinch was a malignant narcissist who considered himself a super scientific genius. Dr. Doofenshmirtz and Wiley Coyote all wrapped up into one. While he never could seem to keep an engineering job for too long, it never diminished his self-proclaiming genius status. He was also a sexually abused Alter boy. His hate for Catholics was his greatest form of self-loathing. Tommy was doomed.

~

As Lilith, Betty and Em ran interference to protect Tommy's ex's affair with the assistant headmaster, they reached out to other character assassins for assistance. Recruited next was Tommy Patrick. He was a twerpy Mr. Mom. As a stay at Home Dad (approximately 2% of the Dad's in America ~ most of them unmarried or widowed Dads ~ usually not married), Tommy Pat was the biggest twit ever born. His days in front of day time TV had made him effeminate beyond his years. His goal of winning the job as the chief gossip at the Cwyane School was his mania. With his wife travelling the world as a high powered attorney, she born her children and then ran out the door. Between nannies and Mr. Mom, she was convinced her boys would be fine. Then at 12, they could be sent off to boarding school like she was. They'd be fine. In the end, her boys would grow to be homosexuals ~ like their Dad. A secret Tommy Patrick guarded successfully his entire life. His hate for a Dad like Tommy was all geared in petty one up man ship and the goal of being revered at Cwyane as being the greatest Dad of them all. Destroying Tommy's reputation was a personal challenge for him.

~

At this point, a principal of any school can halt all the nonsense. In a subtle and polite manner, he or she can diffuse a situation like this rather easily. But, a principal must want to do this. The principal looking to maintain peace and civility can keep the cliques at bay by making all involved aware that children will be hurt by these actions. He or she can perform a little shuttle diplomacy a la Henry Kissinger, and he can build a peace among parents. If Kissinger could foster peace with the Jews and Arabs, how hard would it be for a principal to keep parents from killing each other? That of course relies on one truth. The headmaster must not be a money loving sociopath. He must want to do it. But if he desires to create a school of cliques that he can control with rumor, lies and character assassination, and extort money from wealthy sociopaths like himself, then the cause is lost. See Kissinger won acclaim when his goal of reaching a peace treaty was accomplished.

Unlike Kissinger, Lawrence Berry wanted war. And the Cwyaniac Posse formed to get, one, Tommy Stugats.

~

Lawrenceville Elwood Berry III. Headmaster of The Cwyane Farmhouse School. The head "Master-Baiter". Sociopath. You can almost smell the pseudo-pretentiousness in all those letters found in his name. Born the son of a preacher in the Midwest, Larry Berry knew he was destined for sociopath and narcissistic greatness as he sat in the pew of his father's church at a very young age. At his Father's Church ~ God and Jesus Christ were only visiting. As the sermons on community and life experiences riddled his mind and bounced off the rafters, Larry Berry knew one thing from his father's sermons. Be like us or we'll take you down. It was somewhat different than most church's epistles and definitely alien to the Roman Catholic Church ~ a church that young Mr. Berry grew to see as the Great Satan. After a brief stay in Iowa, Larry Berry found his way to the University of Michigan to study Divinity. Unfortunately, you can't become a pastor or a priest at Michigan, ~ Thank God ~ but you can study religion. Between Wolverine

Football which Mr. Berry loves, and the cold Michigan nights, Larry Berry wanted something more. He wanted to be a hero of mythic proportions. A leader of the world. People genuflecting onto him. As the winter winds of Ann Arbor swirled around him as he walk in the cold night air of campus, Lawrence Berry could see his future before him in the snow. He wanted to run his own small private school one day. Only the simplest people can have the simplest thoughts.

Spurred on by the bow-tied Gordon Gee, next to his father ~ the idol of his life, Larry Berry set forth on a crusade to reach to the top…the top being a principal in a small elementary school. In June of 2013, Gordon Gee was forced out of his college presidency due to racist comments against Catholics specifically the Priests at the University of Notre Dame. It wasn't his first foray into bigotry. His comments about Poles, academic integrity of other schools, state officials, league commissioners and The Little Sisters of the Poor have defined his arrogance and racism. Sadly, he ran a few too many universities in the US. He will not be missed in a growing nation that symbolizes racial diversity and equality. He now is the interim college president at West Virginia University. A school that can and does accept students without even seeing their SAT scores.

As for Lawrence Berry, he married a perky blonde coed 8 years his junior from the Old South waiting 4 years until she reached the legal age. She was the true sociopathic nightmare in his dreams. She exuded the bizarre loud laughter of the fake false front that would motivate Larry Berry to pseudo greatness. With his Narcissist Bride in hand to engender the drama he needed to succeed, L. E. Berry set out to teach at private schools throughout the South. Georgia, South Carolina and Alabama marked his stops through the Old Confederacy as he climbed the educational administrative later to greatness. He need not worry about wealth accumulation. His young wife came from tobacco money in Virginia. It wasn't North Carolina, but it was close enough for him. She lived on the margins of upper society, and he felt he could milk every last penny out of her to succeed. And boy could she lie! But only for a motive or a goal. Usually it was for money. They both were aroused by that fixation. Bt her lies were so monstrous that they could destroy people's lives. She once concocted a lie to destroy Tommy stugats. She was convinced from her days of watching "Fox and Friends" that any man wearing a trench coat in a school must be hiding an automatic weapon intent on a mass killing. Trust me folks. Watching that show will have you putting bars on your windows to protect you from rabiits and pheasants as well! Before she could develop any momentum, L. E. Berry asked his wife to maintain some control. She sounded ridiculous and that would cost them both....money. Little did he know; she was the darkness reaching out from the monetary darkness...

At each stay in his career, Larry Berry acquired titles, awards and mail ordered degrees that made him blush with pride. 2nd place debate team in the State of Alabama, Administrator Entertainer of the Year at the Hope Divine Elementary School fall theater event and Elementary Administrator of the Year in Way Cross Georgia Sectional School District ~ population 350. As the parchments of accomplishments filled his resume, Lawrence Berry grew...in his mind. With a resume full of awards, Master Berry always seemed to gain financially from his job stays as well. New homes, new cars, finished basements, all became normal compensation to him as a gift of the schools he administered and taught. No one was sure how he worked the gravy train, but he did it masterfully. He kept his gifts and always ascended. Then he was hired at the Cwyane School to guide it into the 21st Century. By his evangelical light and might, he would make Cwyane into his own image. His first step at the Cwyane School was to fire his administrative staff ...on Christmas

Eve. He needed his type of God-fearing and money grubbing people. There were roles in the school play to bargain with here. Dead wood out. Blondes in.

~

But first, he would need sycophants. He found them in two forlorn women, the mothers of former Cwyane Students, who just ALWAYS seemed to be around the school! It was as if they never left to get on with their lives. Their children graduated yeeaaarrrsss ago! They just malingered and sat on benches throughout the school watching "their" children walk through the halls in their dream states as their real children had fled them and Cwyane decades ago. As a sociopath, L.E. Berry could see prey, he made these women of lost years and loneliness for family and status, his very own "Frick and Frack". Now JFK had two secretaries on staff in the White House like these women too. They were called "Fiddle and Faddle". But they were there to "service" the President. "Frick and Frack" wobbled down the halls of Cwyane as the "Information Director" and "School Coordinator", and trust me, no one would look at them twice. They both moonlighted at Wal Mart to keep health benefits, so you know how little they were paid at Cwyane for their service to L. E. Berry. But sociopaths like Master Berry can't function without these dilettantes. They are the lost souls who pick up the debris of children's self-esteem as L. E. Berry pursues his dreams of greatness. Like a jack ass looking for a burrow in heat.

~

With each initial hire at the school, it always seemed as if Lawrenceville Berry preferred young, recently graduated blondes. Hot blondes mind you. And preferably dumb. The old teachers with the experience and vigor need not apply. The established teachers who had the classroom management skills gave way to the teachers who coward in the corner as kids began running the classrooms! These perky blondes would worship Master Berry and add to his lustful scenery. Their teaching was average to poor at best. In all honesty, it takes a teacher at least five years to begin to become proficient at their craft. That's why older teachers are always better at the so called "better" private schools. An older teacher knows when a new educational theory is bogus. They hone their pedagogical skills with their talent to teach, their love of teaching, and the careful implementation of new educational theories. Lawrence Berry could care less about those skills. He was the master of his domain. He would choose the blondes that he wanted. They would do what he said. He knew it all. And the parents who he attracted were the ones who could not see through his malarkey, salesmanship and ignorance. You see. These parents didn't have a clue about education either. But they were narcissists. So, they knew everything anyhow. Just ask them. In short, if it was a new educational theory, these parent's would say at their cocktail parties, "Let's implement it so we can be honored as learned parents on the cutting edge of education." L. Berry jumped on this narcissistic parental fear of being socially inadequate like a rhino in mating season. And these sociopaths especially loved the new country club atmosphere being created at Cwyane. New forms of untested education theory to be shared over the patio lunches at the club. Ah.... They had reached the summit. Too bad their kids were becoming educational guinea pigs. Remember whole language?

Now, Lawrence Berry didn't always choose dumb blondes straight out of college. A few of them were very, very bright. The old adage that Blondes are dumb is about as stupid as the racist rants about African Americans. These young and educated women, who also had blonde hair, wanted to implement all of the new pedagogical techniques they had learned at their schools. These researched methods were going to move any school and the country forward into the next century. The older teachers at Cwyane would be their guides because the seasoned teachers would lend their invaluable teaching experiences to critically evaluate these new methods. That is how a well-oiled, blue ribbon school achieves excellence. Well, forget it at Cwyane. These educated women never got the chance. They were moved out of Cwyane with such speed by Lawrence Berry that their diplomas never had chance to develop wall shadows. Only dumb blondes stayed at Cwyane. And Master Berry molded them into his own little harem of ineptitude. They taught whatever The Master told them to teach. Freshly approved by the country club mahjong committee while they lunched at the "club" on "etouffee". If the new stuff failed, dumb teachers covered up their failings by inflating grades. Or they just gave an outrageous amount of homework. Dumb teachers always learned that CYA methodology. The blind parents never had a clue. They weren't in the Cwyane loop. More homework always means the school is harder and better. We paid for the best. Just wait for those SSAT and ERB scores folks. Your kids ain't getting anything special except good looking teachers.

The old guard teachers felt Master Berry's wrath. He pastured many of the older established teachers who built Cwyane's reputation as an academic mecca. He overburdened them with rules and regulations to force them to retire. He catered to the parents who believed their children could do no wrong when they punched, and spit at teachers in fits of rage. Master Berry would force teachers to not only look the other way in terms of discipline to satisfy his parents, but he allowed parents to put in their own discipline in the classroom. One particularly abusive parent was allowed to dictate to a teacher that if her child was acting badly that she should face her desk to the wall of the classroom and isolate her from the rest of the class. "Isolation worked on me" the parent bellowed. So did Zoloft and Valium, but who's questioning the rights of the bi-polar. Worse yet, Master Berry used his own kids to spy on teachers he wanted to get rid of. How could his child possible lie about a teacher's behavior in the classroom? HA! Kids know where the cookie jar is and how to get the cookies. On the complete other hand, God forbid if anyone did that to one of his newly appointed blondes in the classroom. They were protected by Daddy Berry.

The old teachers left in droves. 10 left the first year. 8 the next. Cwyane only had 24 of them to begin with when he showed up on his jack ass. One veteran teacher who had won awards for her curriculum left when he would not accept a fifth grader's science project that was completed at home instead of in class. His reason for the in class assignment was for collaborative and cooperative learning between students. So when little Lord Fauntleroy waltzed in with a project from home that cost his parents $1000 in equipment and another $2,000 for the local college student's work to put it together, his teacher stood his ground and wouldn't accept it. The teacher was removed from the school by L. Berry in exactly twenty minutes. Teachers be damned at Cwyane. Parents with cash rule at Cwyane as long as "The Master" reigns.

Another particularly vile run out of a teacher by Master Berry centered around potty time. The infantile use of the word potty time illustrates the petty and childish behavior of Master Berry. Mrs. Wellis had been at Cwyane for 20 years. Her kindergarten class was legendary for its inclusive projects and annual Halloween Show. But Master Berry had different designs for HIS kindergarten. The Kindergarten Halloween Show will be discussed later. The run out of Mrs. Wellis ended way before Halloween.

~

Now school starts in September and Halloween is but 60 days after kickoff. It was Master Berry's first day of school. He started it off with a flush. Immediately, and in the short time until Halloween, Master Berry set his sights on getting Mrs. Wellis out of Cwyane as his first order of business. Even before Mrs. Wellis could begin teaching the first song of the annual Halloween Show, Master Berry uncovered a secret about her. It came from her rival kindergarten teacher ~ one of Berry's Blondes ~ newly hired kindergarten Sally Tipp.

Sally Tipp was a newly minted teacher better suited to the political pettiness of a sorority house than a school by way of Charlie Brown's sister. But this was Cwyane. They function identically. So Sally Tipp, in her malignant narcissistic way, began to research Mrs. Wellis on that first day in August after she was hired by Larry Berry.

Miss Tipp had a friend in the local hospital network, and with Hippocrates looking the other way, she was able to access Mrs. Wellis' medical records. It was just like accessing sorority pledges' parent bank documents to see if the girls fit the financial profile of her sisterhood. Except for one little matter, it broke the law. Miss Tipp didn't care. She was on a mission to be the number one Kindergarten teacher at Cwyane... Little did she know that Master Berry had that role all locked up from the jump.

It seemed that Miss Tipp unearthed the knowledge of a very serious blatter problem that Mrs. Wellis had been battling recently. It was serious but easily treatable. A few pills and some runs to the lavatory between classes, and she was fine. But with this information, Master Berry struck. On day one, he immediately implemented staff rules for Cwyane. Buried in his hyperbole was a little caveat to teachers that "bathroom breaks" between classes were NEVER allowed. It was fostered under the guise of a gentlemen's agreement to keep teachers in classrooms for security reasons. God knows a pheasant or a ground hog might strike the school with a

9/11 plane strike, but that is the case of the feeble minded watching too much Faux News. No one took the break issue seriously. It became Master Berry's tool nonetheless.

On the first day of school, Mrs. Wellis made a quick potty break. Her students were in art class so she thought the time ideal for a little tinkle. Mrs. Wellis entered the lav unceremoniously. Little did she know, Master Berry was waiting for her. He stalked behind her until she closed the lav door, and he pressed his button. His stop watch buzzed 45 seconds as Mrs. Wellis closed the door behind her only to see Lawrenceville Berry.

"Mrs. Wellis," he barked, "Meet me in my office immediately." As she panicked and hustled to the headmaster office, she had no idea what she had done only that it was grave. The door remained shut for 20 minutes. At its conclusion, the meeting ended and the door flung open. Mrs. Wellis ran from the office crying hysterically and has never been seen again at Cwyane. Master Berry smirked and bellowed to his secretary, "Call Miss Zoid, and tell her to be here tomorrow morning to be the new kindergarten teacher. I'll teach the kindergarten for the remainder of the day." He had become the master of the universe....of this elementary school…. As he headed back to his office to genuflect upon himself, he spotted Miss Tipp. He gave her a knowing wink, and Miss Tipp smiled with her sorority house smile. She too had become the master of her domain as well. These two Alpha Male and Female exert the power of Kings and Queens. Hubris among the hogs. These educational Dons would drink their chocolate milk in the cafeteria with a little bit more gusto today. They had engineered a professional coup. But the real engineering of the hearts and minds came at the kitty not the potty.

But why did Master Baiter need to run Mrs. Wellis out? Well my friends, it seems as if Mrs. Wellis committed the time honored faux paus with a sociopath like Master Berry. She questioned his plan. One question of "why" and the panic set upon Master Berry like a plague of locust on his self-worth. Remember, if you want to destroy a sociopath, hit them where it hurts the most with the truth. Lance their inner self. There they are the weakest. ;)

~

Master Berry LOVED money. Like a hog loves slop. Catering to the very few truly wealthy people at Cwyane, Master

Berry engineered a school fund. He would raise these dollars by selling roles in the school play. 20K to the school, and your kid no matter how theatrically incompetent would be a STAR....in the elementary school play. Ridiculous you say? Not in the minds of the sociopath parent mired at the emotional age of 12 and with a wallet full of Jacksons and Grants. But more about that later. Master Berry had another swindle brewing.

It begins with a wink, and it ends with a Franklin. Autonomous of board of trustee regulation, a pocket full of miracles was filling for Lawrence Berry. With the promise of deceit, L. Berry was raising money…for himself mind you. This fund was filled by the under $1000 donations of his wannabe elite climbers in the parents of Geeks. The checks were written for $999, and the board had no idea about them, and they especially did not know about the cash. Tommy got hooked by Master Berry's charm initially. He donated to him. It was an emergency fundraising to help fix some windows and repair the school furnace. Tommy saw the frigid faces of the little pre-schoolers, and he knew he had to help. Tommy gave Master Berry a large cash donation. He told Master Berry to keep it quiet. He wasn't a bragger. He just wanted to turn on the heat.

Nevertheless, being wise of "street politics", Tommy took precaution. Ever the weary man after spending years in political fundraising, Tommy photocopied each $100 dollar bill before he gave them to Master Berry. It was out of past concerns. It was just to make sure everything went smoothly. Tommy gave Master Berry 75 Benjamin Franklin's and photocopied each one. It was a force of habit for him. Berry wasn't a politician or mobster. Like Jimmy Breslin once wrote, "Mobsters and politicians never could find anything too small that wasn't worth stealing." Headmaster Berry wasn't from that cloth. He was an honesty player. So Tommy believed….and a fool and his money are soon parted.

~

Some people hold raffles and bake sales to raise money for the classroom bulletin board. Some people raise money professionally from large foundations and charities ~ in the millions. At Cwyane, it's a little different. The Annual Cwyane Parent's Ball and Auction is held every year. The gala is one of tuxedos and gowns. It is decorated more lavishly than five to ten student functions together including the school play, all choir concerts or social studies fairs. And by the way, Cwyane Family Parents only.

The pseudo high and mighty work diligently all year long to put on this affair of the absurd at the local country club. They could save a boat load of money having it in the Cwyane Gym, but PLEEEAAASE, we need to show the "class" of our local country clubbers to shine on that night. The club cost 10 Gs just to rent. All the famous and phony at Cwyane gathered two or three times a day at tea, lunch and hors d'oeuvres to create this theater of the absurd. Thousands and thousands of hours of work (?) to create an event that raises perhaps $75,000 ~ after costs ~ 50k. That extra 25K is for the parent get-togethers to PLAN the event. Now taking into mind that there are 300 families at Cwyane and some simple arithmetic, and you get.....$166 a family. Now these are truly the wealthy wannabes. They raise peanuts by serving cashews.

Now if the Cwyane School opened its doors to the City of Cwyane and the surrounding towns, the event would gather at least a few thousand people and some very well healed individuals to boot. The CEOs of numerous large corporations live within 50 miles of the Cwyane School, and would think nothing of sponsoring an event like the Cwyane Auction to the tune of $100,000 each. Also, some of the excluded and exiled families of color (banished by the current Cwyane Hierarchy) might be interested in participating in the Cwyane event. But ignorance and prejudice have kept these people at the farmhouse gate. It is a shame, to say the least. Especially when these people at the gate / "immigrants" are heirs to the fortunes of princes, oil magnates, trust funds and fruit plantations. But when you are Cwyane "shanty", you have the general idea that all people of color are the same people who live in huts around the world. Anyhow, what do you talk about with people like that? Tommy was always convinced that you might THINK OF SOMETHING if their wallets were ready to give. Inclusion is more than an MLK Day Seminar. But truly wealthy people at least have dignity. They went to the private schools where money is raised with class and education is paramount if only to maintain the social order. Cwyane is not that place.

The Cwyane Auction ~ not to be confused with the Parent's Ball ~ began as a method to raise money, and it degenerated into the sale of access for the petty bourgeoisie and their kids at Cwyane. It became rather odd how the more a parent spent at the auction; the more awards and school honors their child received at Cwyane. Of course, buying access is nothing new ~ among the thieves in Washington, DC, Wall Street and Allenwood Federal Prison. When you act like a whore, you are a whore. And L. Berry meant to be the head PIMP of them all.

For sale at the Cwyane Auction, one could find the following. For $300, you buy one seat in the front row to watch the school play. For $500 you buy a parking space next to the headmaster in the front parking lot at the school. You receive a personalized wooden sign denoting that you donated in order to park in a nicer spot than anyone else at Cwyane. Also, let us not forget to mention the parking spaces in the rear of the school cost $250. They offer absolutely the same access to the school, but isn't it much cooler if you could bump into the head master and chat while the whole school is watching? Oh the status bump is ammmmmmazing. Yes, it is as if you are a petty gold digger fresh out of your "id"…I mean "lid" for attention. Oh you can buy parking spots near the curb outside of the school as well for 5 minutes every morning. $100 a minute purchased you direct drop off of your children instead of waiting in line like the rest of the school hoi polloi. Now that is status. Of course, your 5 minute parking time would be timed by the school director of transportation and sanitation. I mean the head janitor. But at Cwyane, everyone needs a status title. In fact, the janitors must wear "Polo" or "AF" collared shirts on the job. Master Berry felt it added to the fact that even though they may be white janitors, they could have some status as janitors. The racism was punishing.

For $400, your child would receive an "escorted" walk with Master Berry to your car on every day that it rained. Master Berry would provide the oversized golf umbrella. For $200, you were permitted to stand 5 feet from the front door of the school to retrieve your child at an early dismissal. For $150, you were permitted to stand 9 feet from that same door. At early dismissal, you could see the assistant sanitation engineer placing yellow tape and orange cones outside the front door to delineate the highly purchased spots. And finally, at the "Great Auction" you could purchase the crème de la crème. Now it wasn't exactly a direct purchase of any item or a parking spot. No it was more of a clandestine bribe. For an undisclosed amount of money ~ rumor had it at 10K ~ a lucky Cwyane student would receive a one week summer acting training session with the "Queen of Drama" at Cwyane ~ The AMMMMMMMMMAZing. ~ Lenore Capulet. Lenore Capulet ~ formerly known as Corpula, she changed her name because she thought it made her sound "fat" ~ was the drama teacher at the Cwyane School. In her AMMMMAZing style, she was AMMMMMAZing at putting on the "AMMMMMAZing" spectacles every year at Cwyane....known as the middle school play. Never had so much effort, time and of course $$$$ been wasted on a childish charade. But this is Cwyane. The High School for Geeks. These over wrought narcissistic parents will spend ANYTHING to keep up with the "Joneses". Needless to say, the musical that year was Gypsy. Only stage mothers allowed.

As the anonymous donation to the one week drama extravaganza training was announced at every Cwyane Auction...And Parent's Ball..., a knowing look would pass through the cheap over-dressed polyester and plastic crowd of parents sporting tacky jewelry fit for a costume jewelry dress up day for the pre-school. The crowd would sneer in petty jealousy as the winning parent's had won the prize. Master Berry smiled as he knew he had raised perhaps $20,000 for the school with losing bids alone. The winners won so much. Their children were headed to "Broadway". The winners believed this fact. The entire room of unsuccessful bidders believed this too. For by winning this bid, their child would of course be.....THE STAR OF THE MIDDLE SCHOOL PLAY.

~

The Annual Cwyane Farm House School "Spring" Drama/Musical/Show. Not to be confused with a middle school play. Never has so much of nothing cost $25,000 or more to produce. It was the show of shows that launched the Broadway and Oscar winning careers of ....ABSOLUTELY NO ONE. In fact, when you starred at this infantile parent hullabaloo, you could rest assured that your acting and dramatic career ended the day you walked off the stage at Cwyane. In short, only the wealthy parents of the most absolutely untalented children would outbid the entire Cwyane High and Arrogant Cabal to land the lead in the play. This is Gypsy via Charlie Kane. Hearst never humiliated Marion Davies with such vigor. At Cwyane unfortunately, someone heard that Taylor Swift went to a small private school near Cwyane, and the race was on to find the next "American Idol" at Cwyane! She would come back to Cwyane as a "star", and Master Berry would solicit a multi-million dollar donation from her for his beloved Cwyane. Too bad, those pipe dreams matched his renovated basement living room. Money does have a funny way of finding the least of us.

These were children being manipulated by adults trying to vicariously live their life's dream while the kid only wanted love and attention. And we wonder why our young girls suffer from eating disorders from psychotic parents pushing them on the ice to skate, on the gym floor mats, the field or the Cwyane middle school stage ~ which doubled as the basketball court and assembly room. Master Berry didn't care. He saw "green". Sociopaths like Berry use children like throw away dish rags. The Cwyane Band played on as Lenore Capulet pied-pipered her little cherubs into dramatic nothingness befit for any forlorn mother of the next Judy Garland. Ms. Capulet also seemed to dress rather stylish after the auction/ball? And to complete the "sleight of hand" the grandparents of the "winning" actor or actress made the contribution to Master Berry ~ in case someone made any legal inquiry as to the selling of the play roles. Little did Mr. Berry know, this information was being ledgered into a little black book for his demise... But Ms. Capulet took the clothing store gift certificates without a word....

Enter Mrs. Buyer. She bought everything for her daughter at Cwyane. Ms. Capulet and Master Berry included. Paid for teacher trips. Paid for administrator gifts at Christmas. Every new technological gadget, dress, jewelry, silly band or novelty care bear. And she bought the lead in the play too.

Mrs. Buyer was a lost Broadway soul. She never had "it" to be on Broadway. And after years of voice lessons, drama lessons, acting lessons, Katherine Gibbs, Lee Strasburg ~ she couldn't fill a seat or get an acting role 100 miles off Broadway. So she became the walking egomaniacal sociopath who disappointed her mother at the age of 10, and she lived with the abandonment of love for the rest of her life ~ of course ~ until she born herself a clone. Little Catie Buyer.

Mrs. Buyer WOULD live her dream of starring on Broadway. She would live it through 8 year old Catie Buyer. Never was so much money spent to augment so little talent. And with a wallet of money passed down from Irish Bootleggers to real estate money laundering, Mrs. Buyer had the cash to buy her dream. Catie Buyer would star on Broadway. Broadway would not elude Mrs. Buyer AGAIN! Catie sat on a folding chair outside the office of Murray Shiefman ~ agent to the Broadway Stars ~ while her mother Mrs. Buyer saw the stars and comets of fame explode over Murray

Shiefman's head and his words of lies. Catie played with her iPhone.

So you have it. The Cwyane School sold its lead roles to its "middle school" play to the highest bidder in order to raise money for Master Berry and fulfill the unreached goals of any of a number of borderline personality disordered mothers. And they bought these roles in a variety of ways. First, in a whisper gossip campaign, Mrs. Berry would inform parents that she befriended (fellow borderlines) that with increased giving to the school that "it always benefited your children." Boy! Did it ever. So the Cwyane Crazy Set dropped money off at the school in baskets. The biggest whore was the "Theatre Arts Director of the School" who ran the play. She would hold pseudo auditions for roles, but everyone knew that Catie Buyer and pals would be getting the best roles. This theatre "wannabe" also started to wear that very fancy line of new clothes at the school while teaching. It became interesting that on a paltry salary of 25K that the Versace and Gucci clothing became her staple attire. Of course, stage crazed parents flooded her desk with gift cards to the tune of 8K. Bribing her was small potatoes. For when Mr. and Mrs. Berry spotted a wealthy grandparent, they latched on to them like vampires with empty bellies. They would have them over to their house for dinner, take them out to eat, send them expensive holiday gifts ~ all at the expense of the Cwyane School ~ which never seemed to ever have enough books or supplies. The direct funnel became a huge contribution to the school play. The reason for this was because Mr. Berry could siphon off the cash donations very easily from the school's books for "miscellaneous" expenses incurred with the play.

Money buying access while their children lay destroyed on the side of the Great White Way. Rich, Stupid and Arrogant are a deadly brew. Sounds like a law firm of divorce lawyers. And you know you are messed up if you enjoy being a divorce lawyer. Destroyed children in a divorce means BIG$ for these bastards. But then again, they never had a pulse to begin with ~ neither did Mrs. Buyer. Sorry Catie.

Each year the Cwyane School would put on the Little Mermaid, Peter Pan or Oliver to satisfy the avaricious and deranged desires of every stage mother who walked into Cwyane to devour Broadway for her own desires. Following on her leach was every miniature Tommy Tune or Judy Garland heading for that 1,000,000,000 to one chance at being the "toast of the world stage" via middle school. Unfortunately these 999,999,999 failures spend their lives on the couches of far too many a shrink. Or they avoid the pain of failing their parents, and they raise kids to destroy of their own. Or, unfortunately, they self-medicate with drugs.

As Tommy would sit in the audience on play night at Cwyane, he would bring a nice flower or small bouquet of daisies to give to Gina to make her smile and tell her that he loved her. Gina loved them. That's how dads and daughters roll. So as Tommy walked by the six Florist Trucks outside of the Cwyane Gym, he kinda felt like his daisies weren't cutting it. Flowers upon flowers streamed out of these trucks in such proportion that The Hot Houses on the East Coast must have been barren all the way to the Netherlands! Tommy gulped hard. Gina would be embarrassed he thought. Then he saw out of the corner of his eye a little girl running. She jumped into the air and Tommy almost didn't catch her. DADDDDDDDDDDDDDDDDD! Gina roared........! These daisies are TERRRIFIC. She smiled at her old man and said, "Dad, you're the best." The $5 Daisy Dad was King of the Hill…again.

But the money whores danced on as the annual Cwyane Musical production gathered money and devoured children's self-esteem. The general public in the City of Cwyane avoided the "Swine Play" for exactly the same reason that they didn't let their children attend Cwyane. It SUCKED. You must understand that no matter how much money you bribe with to get a role, no matter how many voice lessons, acting lessons and dancing lessons you have ~ you can even buy a voice over machine to hide your granddaughter's hiiidddeeoous voice ~ THE SHOW IS GONNA SUCK. And it did, relentlessly, year in and year out. No one saw the great talent agent sitting in the Cwyane Audience. Why? Because *Guffman* wasn't there. It was a hamburger of talent starved spoiled kids all having their parents proclaiming and bribing their way into thinking it was filet mignon.

And as the "Theatrical and Acting Director / Stage Manager" ~ the acting guru of dramatic nothingness freshly minted from her stage disappearance from the civic theatre of Moose Jaw ~ proclaimed how AMAZING! AMAZING! AMAZING! And AMAZING! The Cwyane "Community" Musical performance would be that evening! The Cwyaniac parents discouraged "other" people from the "outside" audience to attend. As the residents of the Cwyaniac "community", the parents of these twerpy children and sociopathic mannequins had their "sand box" all to themselves. MY

GOD, if someone from the outside came to the musical ~ They might bring a gun!" And the band played on.....

They didn't even advertise the Cwyane Play to the City of Cwyane as rows of chairs in the Cwyane Gym sat vacant during the musical. The general consensus was that if we bought the/our roles for our children for the play why should we ALLOW the wretched refuse of the "other" people in the local area to enjoy our greatness. If that was the case, Broadway would fold up and Shakespeare would never be performed again. And so the money flowed into the coffers of Master Berry buy the.....pennies. Yes, he amassed "roles" of pennies from the mattresses of these "wealthy" people. Remember one thing about the pseudo rich at Cwyane. They are doing it all on the cheap. They dress on the cheap, and they give on the cheap. Roles for the Cwyane Play went for a $1000 donation to Master Berry. As if with ten roles to sell in the play and with rolls of pennies coming in by the wheel barrel, The Master could pay his home utility bill and taxes for the year (?) or pay for the damages from the flood in his basement.

But so these pseudo wealthy wannabes sat in the front row of Cwyane to watch their little darlings maul every musical tune and line of Peter Pan and Shrek. The play droned on for hours as lights missed timed, children missed songs and others messed up their cues. And in all, that should be the fun of a middle school play. But the parents of Cwyane paid for more! They paid for "elite" performances from their daring and bourgeoning off spring narcissists. And of course, that's why these wack jobs end up under the petty umbrella of Lawrenceville Berry to begin with. As the kids' voices break in song and the elite acting dreams of these junior high scholars find their way to the trash heap of time as the over-sized trophies of acting greatness get stuffed into the back drawers of their lives, Master Berry counts his pennies on his street of theatrical dreams.

Tommy grabbed a seat near one of the basketball stands to catch a glimpse of the first Act. He was immediately come upon by the "Cwyane Gadfly ~ House Muther" Mrs. Kurns. Mrs. Kurns informed Tommy that he had to move for the "fire marshall". Tommy took one look at the lying cow, and he pointed to the front row of the play seats. "There," Tommy pointed and spoke. And if on cue… crazed parents of the stage elite were pulling folding chairs up to the very front of the stage ~ and blocking two fire emergency exits. Tommy told Mrs. Kurns, "I'd like to see you try to get those people to move." Mrs. Kurns just coward away. The main culprit of the folding chair movement was none other than Mrs. Brown. With complete contempt of social mores, manners of even the pseudo elite, Mrs. Brown placed her chair IN FRONT of her daughter's Grandmother. It wasn't her mom who bribed Master Berry! It was her husband's mother. Needless to say the cat fight of ignorance ensued and the idiocy went to an extreme level. While all this familial drama played out, Poor Liz Brown sang a solo as if she had gravel in James Brown's throat. No, it was not the hardest working man in Rock'n Roll. It was Liz Brown's brother, who always seemed to be stalking her throughout her life????

As the Cwyane Play ended that year in applause, Mrs. Buyer sat miffed beyond consolation. She had sat through every practice of this play for two weeks on her wooden folding chair and had taken copious notes on how to better the play, and it was a FAILURE. The voice dubbing machine didn't work properly and Catie sounded like Lou Rawls on crack. The stage audio system failed throughout the performances, the lighting was mixed up by the 13 year old boys of Cwyane helping out and the Florist forgot 3 of the 7 dozen roses for Catie that evening. Mrs. Buyer was beside her self ~ although having a self wasn't something she ever truly had. Mr. Buyer sat there in his seat in the front row, and quivered in fear of the narcissistic rage about to descend on his and Catie's life. Catie Buyer just sat there and cried. (And unless someone stands up with courage ~ these monsters will continue to devour the children they born and The Master Berry's of the world will simply cash the checks)

~

As the years went by, Tommy endured many petty events designed to run him from the school. At first, when he was rudely treated he lashed back. He yelled and threatened people with a lawsuit or a punch in the mouth. He would say, "Which one is cheaper for you." This was nothing more than a hockey ploy. The hockey player bait's the other player with a dirty play away from the referee's eyes, and when the attacked player (in this case Tommy) strikes back, he gets the penalty. Tommy took an early "roughing" penalty when he was first divorcing. The penalty did not fit the crime. For yelling at Tommy Patrick for blocking him from approaching his daughter at the Halloween Show (which is called interference in hockey), Tommy Stugats received a letter from the attorneys representing the school. The letter written by Dominic Scaremuchi. They always do that ~ ethnic phonies ~. Pit the Italian against the Italian. The Jew against the Jew. The Black against the Black. It comes straight from the divide and conquer Gilded Age. So Attorney Scaremuchi informed Tommy that if he was seen at the school at times other than court approved ones, he would summarily be arrested. ARRESTED. Were they kidding? Tommy truly thought it was a prank at first. He called the lawyer, and after talking with him for a while, tongue in cheek, he started to realize that this was no April Fool joke. Tommy was dumbfounded. But he started to realize what kind of a petty and devious plot it truly was. It was a well-conceived plan to really get him out of the school and eliminate any extra time he could spend with his daughter. Lawrence Berry thought that a recently divorcing, "I-talian", would be under so much stress from his family breaking up that he just might fall for this trap. "You know they can't ever control their emotions like we do," murmured Master Berry. In turn, Master Berry could run Tommy out of the school, curry favor with his most active, money contributing parents, Tommy, Em, Lilith, etc. and be the Master of the Universe. At no time, did any of these people think of the emotional pain that they were inflicting on Gina. How could they? Children are always unaware of how they hurt each other, and sociopaths can make it an art form.

The relentless pettiness continued. When Tommy would drop Gina off for school after his weekends with her, he would drive to the front of the gym and let her off about twenty minutes before school. No one was there at the time. Gina had to lug a book bag, projects and sports bags with her every time. It was a daunting task for any 10 year old. As Tommy would drive off, he could see the "mother hen" FD Tammy Roadway peering at him from behind one of the pillars at the doorway. She was hiding to make sure she could WATCH all. She was CIA / Central Intelligence at Cwyane.

Tammy Roadway prided herself much like J. Edgar Hoover did on keeping dossiers on people. She would barge around the school at all hours picking up little tidbits of information from parents, teachers and others. She stayed away from the janitors because…they were black people…what do you say to them she thought. And as she gathered information all the years, she used it to destroy foes from fellow teachers to parents. She preferred destroying men exclusively. Her man hate came from the fact that she was raped by her father when she was five years old. It was a horrific event to say the VERY least. But instead of addressing the issue personally, she focused on disassociating and on destroying and emasculating any man she held in derision. She stuffed Twinkies down her mouth to the tune of 300 pounds and stuffed men in her pellet bag on her hunts. Her husband fled from her years ago.

~

After he had dropped off Gina on the Monday after their weekend fun, the next day Tommy received a letter in the mail again from Attorney Scaremuchi. The letter was very descriptive. The letter kept telling him that if he continued to drop Gina off at the gym door that the police would be called, and it would be "highly embarrassing" to any young student to see her father taken away in hand cuffs. HAND CUFFS! Tommy thought they were nuts before, but now, he knew they were! So, in a short email, Tommy sent names to every parent in the school, Attorney Scaremuchi, The Master, AD Roadway, etc. BE FOREWARNED it read: That at Cwyane, every parent who drops off their children in a similar fashion as Tommy Stugats was in danger of also being arrested and put in handcuffs! The email list was seventy names long. Tommy also included in the passage, “I am wondering if these other parents have received letters from you concerning a possible police action?” Attached with his email, Tommy sent numerous photos and videos of every type of driving and parking violation performed by Cwyane parents, The Master’s wife and even Tammy Ridgeway, who really liked to park in one of the schools handicapped parking spots near the gym. How did Tommy get all these photos? Well, when you sit in your car, day after day and weekend after weekend with a smart phone in your hand, you have the chance to watch and record a great deal of “road rage”, “crazy drivers” and “psycho mom driving” in the Cwyane parking lot.

After five weeks, there was no reply from Attorney Scaremuchi. One can see how a small mind never sees the bigger picture when they are determined to attack someone in a small way. And pictures speak a thousand words.

~

One particular farce orchestrated by Tammy Ridgeway was the awards ceremony held every year at Cwyane. My apologies. It was called The 55th Annual Cwyane Athletic Convocation Awards, Honors and Accolades Ceremony. It was a ridiculous event with over-sized trophies for undersized achievements for the children of borderlines and narcissists. Never have so many words been used to acknowledge an elementary school event or achievement. This wasn't the Downtown Athletic Club and the Heisman Award. It was more Romper Room on trophy growth hormones. One award (two, one each for each male and female athlete) was given to a student-athlete who exemplified his and her devotion to the team by carrying the equipment to all sporting events for that particular sport. Few can imagine the plight of the under-recognized at Cwyane. And yet, as all the trophies, certificates and honors were bestowed, it became quite apparent to the yawning Tommy Stugats that achievement and worthiness were inversely proportional at Cwyane. And that money contributions to the school greatly increased and were directly proportional for an unworthy child's chance to win an award or get a role in the school play. The correlation was definitive and documented…

With her enmity toward Tommy at a fever pitch, Tammy decided to slight him one more time. When Gina was to receive an award for the most points scored by a basketball player that season, FD Ridgeway didn't let Tommy know that there was a good reason to come to The 55th Annual Cwyane Athletic Convocation Awards Assembly. Although, she made sure Gina's Mom knew with two phone calls and a handwritten note in the snail mail. Tommy was stuck at work, but had he been notified of Gina's award he would have ask for time off at work which his employer would have only too happily given to him. Hell, Tommy's boss loved Tommy so much that he would have probably wanted to come too!

Luckily for Tommy, he overheard some parents discussing what they were going to wear to the Annual Cwyane Athletic Convocation Awards Assembly, and Tommy was tipped off. So in his best shorts, sneakers and Red Sox hat, Tommy made it to the event with time to spare. Begrudgingly, his boss stayed at work. There was a 32 million dollar contract being negotiated, and the boss couldn't let it be discussed in his absence. As the moms and twerps of Cwyane bantered about their makeup and jewelry that they would wear to this late afternoon school event….in the gym, Tommy exhibited the piss and vinegar of a man possessed with contempt for the petty bourgeoisie of Cwyane. When Gina received the award, she waved to her Mom, and she blew a big kiss to her Dad who was standing at the back of the Commons Room. By not being invited with proper invitation, Tommy was unable to secure a ticket for a seat at this standing room only event (20 chairs maximum). But as Gina smiled at her dad, blew him that kiss and ran to his hugging arms, there were few in the audience that didn't realize the un-breakable bond that a daughter has for her Dad. FD Tammy Roadway could only stew in her Queen Ann chair on stage and scowl with hatred. Tommy sent his Boss a selfie photo and video of

Gina with her trophy, and the entire conference room of millionaire businessmen stopped negotiations and exploded in cheers for her. Gina laughed happily as she heard and saw the entire room of "money men" giving her a standing ovation on her Dad's iPad! They could take a break from devouring subordinate debt and clauses for this little girl they all thought. LOL! And Tommy could hear in his mind….

It's only an elementary school, It's only an elementary school, It's only an elementary school…

~

Another petty trick at Cwyane is known as the "turn". Tommy knows it well. The Cwyaniacs are masters at it. Master Berry has been rumored to conduct seminars to teach the "turn" at his home….invitation only. Like the "big donor" dinner he holds at his home for only “big donors” at Cwyane. That might be $200 annual contribution for a couple.

Now, don’t confuse the “turn” with the “twirl” which will be explained later. The “turn” was to avoid with an excuse. Too busy to look at you or say hello because I don’t know who is looking at me, looking or talking to you, and that just might cost me in the Cwyane Hierarchy or gossip notes. And Tommy Stugats was the recipient of the “turn” allllllll the time. It was much like a sorority girl turning her face when she has been caught catting around with a guy and then passing another on the walk home from the first guy’s apartment. It’s called the “walk of shame”. But that was college behavior at its worst, Tommy thought. This was more a “turn” to avoid the character assassin who wants to give you extra gossip.

~

When you start a cult, you need physical symbols. You know…. like a swastika, flags, book burnings… When Master Berry decided that he would take Cwyane into the 21st Century, Buck Rodgers did a 180. Cwyane went back to the 1940's. But unfortunately, instead of rejoining the past of America, Master Berry chose his other favorite nation. And it wasn't Switzerland.

To achieve cult status, you create a "community". Like Manson at Spawn Ranch, you find the weakest minds. You find the most insecure. You find loneliest and the most in need of a friend. Then you prop yourself up as their "father", and it's off to Dachau the others go. You see. Master Berry was an honorable man. He wanted his school to be "his" school. It would be the religion of "Berryanity". But first he needed a symbol.

Master Berry decided that his symbol would first be the rooster. Subconsciously he never recognized his own banty ways and strut around the school grounds as is the case with many narcissists. But to augment his choice of a rooster, he was going to do more than that. Under the pseudo-church inspiration, Master Berry set up a Saturday afternoon "society" gathering place at Cwyane. Technically, it wasn't a "Cwyane" event, but in reality no one but Cwyaniacs attended. He called it the "Farm". Now you can see how the rooster crowed.

Somehow or another, the rooster connived the weak and weary in the school to join him for inspirational readings at the "Farm" every weekend. Interesting, if he had taken Charlie's advice, he would have just flown to Waco, TX and given it all another chance. But unfortunately, Master Berry's view of the world didn't extend past Ohio, and he was more than content to create his cult at Cwyane. Such is the dreams and aspirations of small men.

While Master Berry harangued the faithful, he made a critical error. He tried to extend his cult status into the school curriculum.

They call it the “hidden curriculum” in the pedagogical textbooks, but there wasn’t anything hidden about this lesson. For Master Berry, his goal was to create a church. It’s all he knew. He fashioned himself Peter, The Rock, which the church should be built on. It was funny, but with all his bombast he never had the stones to go to divinity school.

To increase “global awareness,” as The Master wrote home to parents, “Each student will be presented with a “rooster tail gold necklace”. Master Berry was always writing home to parents. The cost of the postage was astounding. Wasn’t email supposed to save trees? Whether it was Summer or Easter Break, The Master would drone on with some type of flimsy prose about the chirping of birds or the destiny of the leaves in the breeze. He fashioned himself the sermon writer. Week in and week out, a hymnal or missile would make its way into the mail box of the Cwyane faithful. The Blondes would swoon at his wisdom, and the pews would be filled at The Farm. With regards to the “rooster tails”, Tommy immediately thought Yankee Doodle and Macaroni, and nearly pissed himself laughing.

As Tommy continued to read the letter sent home, Master Berry proclaimed, "At each Cwyane event, this beautiful Cwyane symbol SHOULD be worn by every Cwyane student to symbolize our dedication and admiration of the Sun rising." Tommy could never imagine where Berry came up with this shit, but he sure spent a great deal of time on it. Berry was always pontificating on some kind of free flow thought that resembled more of an Acid trip with the Osmonds than anything of substance. Preachers can drone on with the most ridiculous nonsense....or chicken feed, Tommy thought.

Well, a funny thing happened on the way to the Supreme Court. It was the word SHOULD. You see when the founding fathers decided that we SHOULD ALL have the free exercise of our drivel that came from the most widely assorted assholes in the history of the world, they placed one caveat on the matter. They insisted that it be with the, "...FREE exercise thereof..." NOT SHOULD! A child might choose to wear a rooster tail necklace, but they didn't have to do it. It is more a compulsion than a request unless of course you are on a FARM. (?) Needless to say, the faithful complied. A very few number of parents with open minds decided to resist the order. They had seen enough. They received the relational bullying of the faithful, the dirty looks and the shunning appropriate to NOT following a Master Berry order! They left the school. Cwyane became more White and Protestant as the case may be. "So they left," said Master Berry ~ it was his goal to begin with to weed out the thinkers. Hence, the pigs stayed, and Monster was sold for glue. And of course the head pig was Master Lawrenceville Berry.

~

As the wheels of justice turn slowly, one day a short note was sent to Master Berry. It was from the ACLU. The Animal Cruelty Liberation United. The request was short and sweet. Please stop "imploring" students to wear "rooster tails" as it may encourage them to assault the fowl in the local area in pursuit of dedication to this symbol. Unfortunately, a nearby farmer had had his twenty-five roosters killed recently, and the only thing taken from the animals was their rooster tail feathers. Master Berry laughed at the note. His SS was coming together nicely. It was just another random act of "Cwyane-ness". Unfortunately, The Master was none too happy when he received a certified letter from the ACLU asking him to investigate the recent rooster mutilation and his "Rooster Tail dedication ceremony" held at Cwyane. "It seems to have a possible link to recent events in the area," the note read. The note went on to state, "A recent FARM weekend meeting service at Cwyane may also be related to this incident, and we would greatly appreciate your clarification on this matter." Master Berry went dark. He turned to his staff and was about to throw the letter onto the ground to create a snake to devour these tree hugging malcontents. But then he thought, "That was too much of a direct act." He would be more surreptitious.

It's only an elementary school, It's only an elementary school, It's only an elementary school…

Tommy walked into the local mini mart for some chips, and he stood in line to pay. He was half salivating over the kettle made wonders when a voice from behind him whispered none too quietly. "You're one of those *Swine*, aren't you?" crowed the voice. Three other people in the store looked at him. The tension seemed to instantly build. Tommy wasn't exactly sure how to deal with the situation. He appeared to be dealing with one townie, but could he be surrounded by other raptors? It was dark outside. Should he chance a quick foot race to the car? Tommy really wanted those freak' in chips! So he decided to turn around to face the music, and the punch in the mouth.

~

As he turned and clenched his fist, he heard the guy behind him say, "Yeah, I thought it smelled like pork in here." Tommy looked at him. Then in a sudden burst of courage and anger he spewed forth his retort. "Listen asshole, I've got an ex-wife keeping my kid hostage in that place so she can relive the high school experience that she never had. I get shit from all of them, and I really don't need it from your side of the street. I just want to buy my f'n chips." You coulda heard a pin drop.

In retreat, the local yokel stammered, "Yeah buddy, no problem, chips, yeah, buy your chips." Tommy turned around and miraculously went to the front of the line. Three people moved out of the way for him. Tommy thought he might use this again sometime soon. As he walked out of the store with coins in his hand, a small tremor let loose in the City of Cwyane. There were cracks in Master Lawrenceville Berry's Kingdom of Cwyane ~ Swine. The word would now spread amongst the citizenry like wildfire. There was dissent at the Swine Farm of Cwyane.

~

It might be better to call it a disease. It began as a high school clique, but in later years it develops more into a gaggle, and perhaps more appropriately ~ a law firm. I'm talking about soccer moms. Tommy calls them "hamsters". He says they run all day long on their wheels, and they don't really accomplish anything. You know them. The drive gigantic SUVs to protect their children while they are really terrorizing everyone else on the road. They wear baseball hats with no teams on them and pony tails sticking out the back. They cackle sweet nothings all day long, and dangling whatever bracelet they have on their wrist. If given the choice between the two, pardon to Dr. Seuss, I'd pick the sea-sick crocodile.

With little going for themselves, they find the need to herd. They graze on vegetables and the newest fads. Medicine intrigues them. They buy every new TV advertised elixir and pill they can find, and they test them on their poor, horse-broken spouses. Pharmaceutical companies know this and market to them accordingly. The myth of the cougar hunting young men is alive and well with these overstuffed, middle age women because in reality they aren't very good looking, and why would an 18 year old buck want to have them over a sweetie their own age? But they can spread their venom when they desire. Emasculation is their dream date.

One such Cwyaniac hamster was "Tits". She was called "Tits" because that's about all she had, and she flaunted them accordingly. Surprisingly, she was hated by only a few fellow hamsters. The true "A" cup bunch were jealous. But as those triple "D's" bounced around the Cwyane courtyards, her identity mirrored her bra size.

Tits found it necessary to wear very low cut blouses, and tight skirts. The view of her chest was clear. Her cleavage looked like Mojave Point, Grand Canyon. For the over stimulated sixth-grade boys, she was a wet dream. To the Dads, she was eye candy. To her enemies, she was a motor boat and a threat.

Tits immediately took to Tommy. He admired her lungs, but he was married at the time, and discretion and fidelity need to go together he thought. But that didn't stop Tits. For Tommy, he enjoyed how she would rub her "tits" on his arm when she walked by in close quarters. But don't let that fool you folks, distinguished married gentlemen like Tommy don't sink the ship swimming after a big titted mermaid. No sir, class is rooted in ethnicity, and Italian men never let two sides of their world every cross. One night stands are not wives, and you don't necessarily eat where you crap. ;)

~

Tits ran to Tommy every time she saw him. She flouted her breasts for him. She jiggled them for him when she talked to him, and she always seemed to drop a pencil or a sippy cup when she was standing next to him. Tommy would find himself in a difficult position especially wearing shorts. He would constantly attempt to flee her presence, but that was her true game. To use those tits to get anything she wanted. They were the actions of the truly worthless. And Tits really wasn't worth a shit. Of course the evil eyes of Cwyane reported all this to each other in an attempt to convince their husbands that they all needed a boob job. And they all sagged....and they did need them.

~

So Tits was the tits! At least she thought she was. She boobled around talking in the lingo of the hamsters ~ "Yaaa Think?", "Oh, that's a good thing", Thhhhhank yoooooooooou." and "Did you see Oprah yesterday?" She had it all Cwyane. But the one thing she did best was flirt. She would bat those eyes and booble those things to the point of nausea. All the men at Cwyane ~ and I mean the twerps and all ~ googled at Tits, and I don't mean an internet search. She drove the male hormones crazy at Cwyane. And of course, the only one "on" to her flirting act to piss off every woman at Cwyane was Tommy Stugats. He saw those motor boats, and he fled. No reason to deal with that silicone, and piss off my wife he thought. And of course, it did anyhow. It happened to him because Tits got pisst. Because Tommy ignored her for the fidelity of his marriage, she had to do something. So she concocted a monstrous lie of how Tommy attempted to maul her at a 6th grade choral concert. She cried and sheepishly told EVERYBODY at Cwyane that she was not coming around to the school anymore because she was sooooo afraid that Tommy would do it again.

Now Tommy was in deep shit. Not only did every woman in the place hate him for not "flirting" with THEM, but he was also the most hated gent among the twerps. The twerps resoundingly shunned him as a pathological rapist. "How dare Tommy cheat on his wife? With our "Tits" to boot!" they howled. Then it got worse. They started to tell their children in the school to be careful of Tommy because he might try to attack them. "He could be a pedophile rapist too." they bellowed. And it got worse. One day Tommy's darling Gina came to him crying saying, "Dad, do you like Mrs. ~ because of her boobies." That was the last straw for Tommy. While the whole matter was now being used by Tommy's STBX (Soon To Be eX-wife) to turn the school parents against him as she frolicked with the assistant principal, Master Berry couldn't help himself but to step in to use the situation for his advantage. It was too perfect.

When children are used as pawns in a country club game of gossip and shunning, they grow up to be the same type of miscreants as their parents. Parents talk about other people in front of their children as a mechanism to tell them what to do while not doing anything at all. The children dutifully parrot the hateful pettiness to their friends and before you can say The Menendez Brothers the children disrespect the targeted parent or the teacher or the other child. These children don't say excuse me, or thank you or please because they have never seen their parents do it. They harass targeted parents by incessantly trying to talk to them in a condescending voice that only their parents could instill in them. It is a sense of entitlement from an over inflated sense of pseudo-wealth and status that these nouveau riche seem to think they have acquired. In a small suburban town, wealth can seem to be much more than it really is until they try to buy a soda for their kids in

New York City. And then the reality of their financial nothingness kicks them squire in the ass. And their children's rudeness is nothing more than the reflection of their parents' faux societal position. Let them eat cake is their mantra when they are only allowed to devour the cupcakes of status instead.

~

Master Berry summoned Tommy to a meeting. He made it sound like it was just a "how are you" or a "get a cup of coffee" type meeting, but his real agenda was much more nefarious. You see, Master Berry planned to banish Tommy from Cwyane. Because in his mind, Tommy was a threat.

It's only an elementary school, It's only an elementary school, It's only an elementary school…

The threat of Tommy Stugats caused great fear in Master Berry. It all started with his ego and ended in cash. Master Berry couldn't help himself to the cash. He suffered from Greed ~ one of the seven deadly sins and a disease suffered by all social climber wannabes at Cwyane. And, five years before these meeting, Tommy gave Master Berry 75 Ben Franklins for use in the school. Tommy wanted to help with the refurbishing of the old leaky bathroom for students. Master Berry had other ideas. Master Berry believed it was his to use as he fit….And he did. He took the Ben Franklins ~ all 25 of them, and had a nice little sojourn to the beach with some of his newly hired "blondes". He told the school that the trip to the beach was really a training conference to observe the inner workings of the Ocean City School District. Oh those inner workings were observed all right. Right down to the trip to Victoria Secret to purchase gifts for his harem. While Master Berry enjoyed his Ben Franklins, he was now prepared to rid himself of any entangling alliances with Tommy. No one would believe a "rapist/pedophile" after Master Lawrenceville Berry got finished with rumor bashing him from the grounds of his beloved Cwyane. Tommy thought about all kinds of things when he approached Master Berry's office door that day.

As the two got right down to business, Tommy asked, "Can I at least get a cup of coffee?" Master Berry retorted, "We don't have time for that." Just then two men in suits came into the room. "These are members of the Cwyane legal team who want to sit in our meeting." said Berry. Little did Tommy realize that Master Berry put on the speaker phone so his secretary and school business manager could illegally listen to the conversation and be able to testify against him. The secretary had her phone taping everything that was said. Richard Nixon was smiling somewhere.

"Legal team?" Tommy gasped surprisingly, "What legal team ~ and for what?" "Mr. Stugats, unless you allow these men into our meeting concerning Mrs. ~ and your unwanted advances to her and the children at Cwyane, I am sorry but I will have to ask you to leave Cwyane permanently." Master Berry proclaimed.

Tommy glared at him. Tommy's eyes went to a deep black. You couldn't see any whites in his eyes. He smelled a set up when he sniffed one. As Master Berry smirked at him with the power of Zeus in his clutches, Tommy excused himself from the room. "This game has just started. You better ask your Ben Franklin's where this is going to all end up Mr. Berry." Tommy told him as he slammed the door behind him leaving off such a ripple of sound that half the school shook. As he left, Tommy could see the business manager and secretary listening to and then fumbling with her speaker phone. "Didn't think I knew you were listening, did you two?" Tommy left out a final harangue. "I'll be seeing you at the depositions." Tommy sauntered out. The worm had turned….. We'll get back to all this later.

~

Let me describe "The Bobblehead" (Not to be confused with the Booblehead, if you're scoring at home). We'll call her "Bobbles." Bedecked in "Life is Good" everything, LL Bean outerwear and massive faux diamond earrings that pull her ears down to her knees much like her breasts at this advancing 40 something age, she can be found at any private school. She is that high school or sorority girl who married well. She found that doctor or lawyer. She never found herself, abstract thinking or her maturity, but she found the ATM machine. Armed with her check book and her "Life is Good" cap, she is CWYANE. She shows money, but she really is done up on the cheap. Her ability to thrive at a school like Cwyane is directly related to how many groups she can belong to, committees she can join and snacks she can supply. She coordinates the after game snacks at all the sporting events, she hands out programs at all the school program concerts and she passes out Lilies at Easter Break like an angel / Poinsettias at Christmas. To Tommy she always seemed to be more like a church usher gone MAD with power! She is always fake smiling trying to keep up appearances, and ultimately is as fake as her smile. And the one overwhelming attribute that she has is that her head is built on a swivel. Her head can spin, and bounce and bobble whether she is thrilled, melancholy or pisst to a point where Linda Blair would be jealous. Her head just keeps shaking. I mean it bobbles. You can hear he say, "Ohhhhhhh yeeeessssss!" as her head moves and bobbles in unison to the hhhhs and eeees in her words. It truly is an art form.

Not only does the bobble head have a head that bobbles, but she always has a pony tail that can keep pace with her words and her head. There really should be an Olympic Sport for such skills. Nevertheless, there is not one at the Olympics, but at Cwyane Olympics it may be proposed to Master Berry. And in this school with Mommy and me Pilates, Make your own fragrance night, Grass growing through meditation seminar and of course Master Berry's book club, the Olympic Sport for Bobbling is never too far away from reality at Cwyane. Master Berry always seemed to have extra money for these seminars or activities ~ like the Cwyanian Olympics, and no one ever knew how he did it. Tommy did.

~

The sad demise of "Bobbles" came on that day that she attempted to go to Cwyane without her face. Mascara and rouge sales skyrocketed at drug stores that littered the drive home for many Cwyaniac moms that day. Unfortunately for Bobbles that day, she wanted to quickly pop in and pop out of Cwyane with the hope of picking up her Japanese Cherry Blossom sprouts from the school store only to quickly vanish in her Escalade to her bathroom and her face life support table. Unfortunately, it didn't work out that way.

As poor Bobbles did find her way out of the school unscathed, she didn't realize that Carly Dunnanhan had parked just a little bit too close to her bumper. Nightmarish parking behavior is a staple for Cwyane parents. Narcissism never sees a traffic sign or law it didn't ignore. As Bobbles threw it into reverse to make her get away, she nicked Carly's BMW station wagon (leased, not bought). It was but a tiny scratch. I've seen better marks on hockey player's face. But for the darling Miss Bobbles, it was much worse than that. It turned into her Cosmetic Waterloo.

As for the fact that it was the beginning of school, everyone was walking their children into the school, and saw the "near death" collision. A large crowd assembled around Carly's scathed rear bumper. The mothers gawked, and the children howled. Bobbles was beside herself. She was crying profusely as every woman in the crowd gazed at the damage. "Oh my God look at her," they gasped, "Look at her." "I've never seen one like that." "It's horrible." Everyone in the crowd seemed to groan in concert. It was a choir of cat calls. But it wasn't a car scratch they were crowing about here.

No, no sir it wasn't. Always quick to be everything, everywhere to everyone and always the center of importance, Master Berry held Bobbles in his arm. "Now, Now, Mrs. Insany, there is no need to cry." Bobbles looked up at him and said, "Don't you see?" She was in utter despair. "They aren't looking at the car!" Master Berry shoo-ed away the licensed Swain Photographer as he had lurched forward to serve the paparazzi void. "They are looking at me." Bobbles barked with ferocious Narcissistic pain. Unfortunately, she was right. Never at a loss for a power grab, Master Berry said, "Let us say a prayer." Three Farm Zealots knelt to the ground. It was vomitous.

On that fateful day, the grim reaper of vanity came calling for Bobbles. The Avon Lady had disappeared into oblivion, and Bobbles was left without her pancake makeup. Bobbles was not beautiful and bouncy in her well made up face anymore. She was the sea hag in all her glory. And now the whole world could see, at least the Cwyane World looked. As the cell phones clicked photos and videos of her face, and it immediately went viral on Twitter, Instagram and YouTube, Bobbles the bobblehead was now relegated to the trash heap of lost faces. Her age had been hidden for years, but now it was as exposed as the garish Sun. The other mothers trembled with fright. They were always afraid of something, but this time they were in fear of Father Time. That could have been I they fretted in whispers. Drug store stocks soared on Wall Street as money found its way into another fine Cwyane mess. Master Berry triumphed none the less. He was able to get three parent Farm Zealots to genuflect to him….

~

Humans much like animals are naturally gregarious. Animals herd. De Tocqueville wrote about associations in democracy. And Cwyane would have its sorority gang too. And with black balls in hand, there was born an interesting clique at Cwyane. There is one somewhat like this everywhere, but at Cwyane it borders on the obscene. They are known as the clones ~ they act, dress, talk, fart and all seem to smell the same. Corporate America markets to these women like a moth letting out her essence. Like the cheerleaders on Glee. They always travel in herds, and they always seem to be whispering for a few moments with the determination on their faces of foreign leaders at Geneva. Then, they blurt out ridiculous cackling laughs which deflate their credibility as members of the diplomatic corps. Schottenfreude of the absurd

~

Tommy had an ever increasing problem at Cwyane and it wasn't just Master Berry. It was Lilith, Betty and Em. And to this trio, add "Frick and Frack". "Frick" was a little meatball of a women with one gay son who she hovered over like the "Huey" she was, and her two other boys were the supreme Bullies of Cwyane that she ignored and abused with a strap in the darkness of her closed front door. You'd be surprised how many of these perfect Cwyaniac parents use the strap with great alacrity in their parenting repertoire. Master Berry once attempted to conduct "How to Parent" seminars at Cwyane in his attempt to bring his cult in sync with the current research The seminars quickly dissolved when attendance of the narcissists parents was few, and the first comment from a Cwyaniac parent was, "So what do I do with my wooden board of education?" The old gag gift was greeted with great silence among the parental brethren as the mother quietly sat down in confusion when there was no reply to her inquiry.

But the "Hueys" were different. "The Helicopters" are what is kindly used as the defining word for mothers who spend their every waking day "hovering" over their sons like copters in an attempt to enmesh into them in pursuit of themselves. They were called "Hueys" in Vietnam. They are the mothers who live through their sons. They make their sons. They make these boys into pathetic momma's boys. Many of them become so effeminate that they become something every Dad fears.

"Frack" was Frick's buddy whose mother in law came from a very good education at the Yale University Theater School and Frack's mother had a reasonably successful career on Broadway. But now the anonymous "Frack" was going after the big fish. To her, Cwyane was a step up above all her relatives.

We all lose track of reality on a roller coaster. Frack's bi-polar disorder was the reason for hers. As a long standing family member of the "stage", Frack knew all the Mafiosi in the known world. Every time she even remotely believed that she had seen a person of Italian descent she knew they were La Cosa Nostra! And she knew Tommy Stugats was a mobster! Her theater instincts told her so. And he liked guns too. In fact, as I told you before, at the school play, Tommy was asked to move his seat by Mrs. Kurns. Well, Frick was not to be out done by her. Frick asked Tommy not to sit in a certain seat at the Spring Choral Concert "because it was the Fire Marshal's request…AGAIN!" Of course, at the same time, parents were pulling folding chairs and expanding the front row near the stage so they could have "premium seats" to watch their cherubs act before they headed to the Lincoln Center! Later, Tommy would find out that the main reason Frick wanted to move him was that he was being accused by Master Berry's wife that underneath his London Fog coat that Tommy Stugats was carrying an AK47! Now that's a mobster! Tommy heard the rumor, and laughed uncontrollably as the gossiping mother who informed him stood looking at him in stunned silence. She thought he was "packing" too! Tommy looked her straight in the eye and said, "Not for nuth'in. That's not how we do it." She ran in terror! Tommy convulsed into hysterics.

~

The game that the "Freak Five" (as Tommy referred to them as) were to play on Tommy was a hybrid of "Shun for Fun". This hybrid was more a "Shun and Done". Through a relentless whispering campaign and back turning, the Freak Five informed nearly every parent at Cwyane that they all needed to rid themselves of the wife beating, pedophile Mafiosi named Tommy Stugats. Many parents who they whispered to had no idea who Tommy was. That really didn't matter. It only mattered to Tom Stunard ~ another Cwyane Parent in exile ~ who only wanted to get his daughter a good head start in her education by enrolling her in the Cwyane Kindergarten. Mr. Stunard was confused with Mr. Stugats. He took a brutal shunning. He left Cwyane in a heartbeat that June with the impression that Cwyane Parents were brutally psychotic in their shunning and rudeness! Little did Mr. Stunard know, but he gave Tommy Stugats a brief reprieve.

As the Freak Five worked their treachery, other Cwyane Parents wanted to join them. You see, they wanted to be a part of the “in” crowd. When one of the Freak Five would see Tommy talk to someone at Cwyane, they would quickly slither up to that person of that moment, at some Cwyane event or after school function, and let their venom out about Tommy. Smiles for Tommy would be quickly replaced by scowls at him from the newbies. Master Berry and his wife were the most notorious gossips and shunners. They took care of the staff and school administration. They lent their hand to swaying numerous parents as well. It was for the good of Cwyane.

One such twist, twirl and turn did bother Tommy a lot. He had befriended one of the few African American families at Cwyane because he thought at least they might talk to him because they were being treated like chattel at the school already! They were only at Cwyane to avoid a civil rights problem for the school. Cwyane was desperately trying to recruit minority students ~ all this being the case while the Town of Cwyane was 47% minority??? A few children of color at Cwyane were on a scholarship to avoid Title IX & X, and any other amount of state laws.

So the husband of this family hit it off with Tommy. They talked football. Joe being a Cowboys fan always seemed to engender some sort of tease by the Philadelphia Eagle Fan in Tommy's soul. They horsed around laughing about stupid things, and generally enjoyed each-others company. The fun didn't last long.

In short order, it was devised that when anyone of The Freak Five saw Tommy at Cwyane or an event at the school, they would turn their backs on him. They would literally physically turn their backs to him. It became almost like a waltz to Tommy. Imagine, entire rooms full of people turning their backs on you in a gallant twirl. Tommy found it refreshingly comical. He even noticed a breeze. The problem was Gina didn't. It hurt her feelings because all the kids at Cwyane at the urging of their parents began to swirl on

Gina as well. The little girl was heart-broken. Call it Social Exclusion if you are scoring at home. Gina thought these people cared about her. She did have some strong little friends who stood by her, but the damage was done. Gina feared the times that her Dad was coming to a concert or an art show because of the swirling. She told him once not to come. This broke Tommy's heart. The Freaks smirked. They were accomplishing their goal for Master Berry. Gina really didn't mean it. Her Mom told her to do it. Dr. Spock rolled over in his grave.

~

Here are a few examples of "Shun and Done". The Field Trip with the Freak Five. Gina was terribly excited that her Dad was coming on a field trip as a chaperone. What kid isn't?! I'm sure everyone remembers these times. You are thrilled your parent is there, and you're very proud of them. This greatly disturbed the Freak Five in Tommy's case.

The bus that day was heading to the Liberty Bell in Philadelphia. It was a short trip, and two luxury buses were rented for the excursion. Most schools use yellow school buses for these events, but in Cwyane's arrogance only a luxury liner would do. That's $2,500 for the day. Ridiculous.

As the buses began to fill up, Gina and Tommy hopped on to the first bus before anyone else. As Gina's friends bounced and giggled into their seats, Gina was thrilled too. Tommy sat with them. A chaperone's job he thought.

Gradually, "Shun and Done" was implemented….

When all the Freak Five et al climbed the stairs to be seated on Bus One, they descended on Tommy in short order. They spotted Tommy on the bus, and they proceeded to "twirl" and make for Bus Two with a smirk on their faces as they caught Tommy's eye in the window. Luckily, Gina was so thrilled to be playing with her friends that she never noticed that the parents were all congregating on Bus Two. That always seemed to be the case each year that went by at Cwyane. As Gina and her friends got older, Tommy seemed much cooler to them than the other parents. The kids couldn't understand why parents always said the nastiest things about Gina's Dad at the dinner table. Then it dawned on everyone on Bus 1! They were jealous of Gina's Dad.

Imagine that, Bus One: 32 children and Tommy and Bus Two: 39 parents and three children. And the children on Bus Two were pisssssseeedddd! As the teachers looked at the disparity in chaperones, they entered Bus Two to recruit parents for Bus One. "Parents, please help us on Bus One with chaperoning the children. Most of them are on it," One teacher asked politely. Not one person moved. The Freak Five smirked. A few parents squirmed in their seats, but did not volunteer. Parental subservience, Relational

Bullying and loyalty to “Shun and Done” had been accomplished. But didn’t they all think that Tommy Stugats was a pedophile? LOL!

The teachers shook their heads, and proceeded to Bus One. Luckily, three parents who had come late and who genuinely liked Tommy (including Joe) got on the first bus. They bordered Bus One on the teachers’ desperate request for help. The Freak Five looked on and committed themselves to dealing with those parents later....

The Liberty Bell trip was a blast for Tommy and Gina. During the field trip, Tommy stopped at a vendor outside the Liberty Bell and bought all the kids soft pretzels and mustard. The Freak Five FLIPPED! Tommy had violated the nutritional gluten free diet calendar for the day. Gluten was everywhere. Hives, sneezes and leprosy would abound immediately they feared. As Gina and her friends galloped around the Liberty Bell Shrine and ate soft pretzels and mustard until every kid’s shirt was stained beyond hope of saving it in the washer, The Freak Five was mortified, and their cohorts twirled on Tommy and the children thrilled at all the fun. "Man buddy, you made my day!" thanked the Vendor! One of Gina's friends said, "Gina. Your Dad is soooooo cool. I can't figure out why my mom keeps spinning away from us?" Gina smiled. Tommy heard the comment at a distance. Game over. Gina was happy. Happy Kid is job one in the world of sane parents.

But today's turn of events was the exception rather than the rule. Mostly, the tension between Tommy and the Freak Five et al was as thick as mozzarella on a deep dish pizza. On one very, very sad occasion, the parents attending the Halloween Parade began to turn their backs not only on Tommy but on Tommy's mother as well. Gina's grandmother had come to school to enjoy the festivities with Gina that day. That was the day when Gina grew up years beyond her age, and developed a stronger bond to Tommy and his mother that seemed to be cast in stone.

As the swirling began at the Halloween Party, Tommy's Mom tried to catch up with a conversation with Joe. She had enjoyed chatting football with him along with Tommy. On the few times she came to the school, they chatted with ease. But on Halloween, the Ghoul in Joe made a scene. All Saints day was the next day, and Joe was going to bedevil souls now. As Tommy's Mom approached him, Joe ignored her. Literally, he looked right through her. The Freak Five smiled at Joe. Then, Joe twirled like a seasoned veteran. Tommy saw this. And as Joe continually avoided conversing with his Mom, Tommy over heard one parent remark, "Don't you think that Joe will be a fine treasurer on the Cwyane Parents Board of Advisors?" All of sudden, Tommy got it. Joe was bought and paid for by the Freak Five Political Apparatchik. Joe's back finally came full circle on Tommy's Mom, and she was shocked and hurt. Schottenfreude loomed. Some smirks and cackles could be heard from the peanut gallery, and Tommy quickly went up to his Mom to break the ice storm. Gina saw this too. She then spoke from a place in each of us that beholds the truth from Heaven. Gina put on her gown, wings and halo, and embarked for a sojourn around the room. When the room of diabolic parents became briefly quiet, Gina blurted out strongly, "I love you Grammie!" Grammie went from sad to joy! Shottenfreude her ass! Keep your Nazi bullshit to yourselves. (Tommy's Mom could go to the curb with her language with the best of them, but she chose to refrain from it in proper company ~ and this wasn't proper company anymore!)

Before Tommy's Mom began to curse like a sailor, Gina began to go to every person turning their backs on her grandmother and ask them, "Why are you being mean to my Grammie?" These people of 40 or better were stymied in their adolescence. They froze. Their inner selves were driven into submission. They started to move away from this three foot little angel like she was the Armageddon and The Second Coming all wrapped up into one. They had been exposed by a child, and the child in all of them reared their heads in personal disgust at each of them. As some parents sheepishly made their way to Grammie because they had felt the truth spear them in their heart. Gina's grandmother just shook her head. Gina hugged her Grammie with unbridled love. Gina chimed out to anyone in ear shot, "I love my Grammie. I love my Grammie." A tear welled up in Grammie's eyes.

Tommy helped gather Gina's belongings at the end of the Halloween Day fun, and he, Grammie and Gina made for the door. The Freak Five couldn't help but try one more swirl, but Gina's Mom told them to stop too. Grammie said to them, "Hasn't Gina shown you enough?" Whatever motherly instinct Gina's Mom had left stood up to protect her daughter. She shook her head to stop them as well. As Gina left, she kept saying, "I'm sorry Grammie. I'm sorry Dad." Tommy grabbed her and hoisted her above his head. He smiled at her, and she laughed! "YOU ARE THE GREATEST DAUGHTER IN THE WORLD!" Tommy told her. "And you are the greatest granddaughter ever!" his mom chimed in.

“Let’s get a slushy.” Tommy announced. Gina became ecstatic! Nothing like a slushy to save the day. The Freak Five had made their last stand.

~

Tommy pulled up to the mini mart gas station desperately in need of gas. He made sure that he avoided the chips again to avoid that form of gas as well. As he moved to the pump to punch in his life story, he caught a glimpse of someone approaching him. He looked quickly, and it was that same asshole who had given him shit the month before. Tommy stood him up as he came forward. “Don’t give me anymore shit or I’ll pull out my pipe and crack your skull!” Tommy yelled. The man stopped dead.

As the confrontation reached stalemate, the man spoke, “Listen, don’t do anything crazy. I just want to apologize for yesterday. I’ve asked around about you and people know about the crap you are taking at Cwyane." Tommy glared at him. He was so jaded at the prospect of someone being nice or classy that he stood his ground fiercely. The man smiled a crooked grin, but Tommy's sixth sense told him that this guy meant his apology with all sincerity. Tommy gradually defrosted. The man extended his hand and said, "I'm Todd. I own the *Radio Room* at the Mall. I am truly sorry too."

They shook hands as gentlemen. Something unheard of at Cwyane.

In fact, manners take a holiday at Cwyane. From parents to teachers to students, flatulations and eructations explode in proper company with a deafening silence to follow. Yes, I said farts and burps for the English majors. By definition,

flat·u·lence (flăch′ə-ləns) *n.*

1. The presence of excessive gas in the digestive tract.

2. Self-importance; pomposity.

The American Heritage® Dictionary of the English Language, Fourth Edition copyright ©2000 by Houghton Mifflin Company. Updated in 2009. Published by Houghton Mifflin Company. All rights reserved. The perfect definition for Cwyane thought Tommy Stugats.

Flatulence: to emit stomach gases through one's anus and/or mouth. The high and mighty of class and sophistication at Cwyane, pass gas without even the proper dignity or manners to excuse one's self. Class does not equal Cwyane. They are so narcissistic at Cwyane that first, they don't even recognize their flatulence in the presence of others, and second, "HOW DARE!" they ~ The Cwyane Elite ~ have to apologize for anything… ever! So the excuse me(s), pardon me(s) and "I'm sorry(s)" never see the light of day. But the smell of air fresheners often permeate the halls of Cwyane. You might think that manners and other so called "virtues" might be well understood behavior at Cwyane. But they are not. It's beneath them. When you sell parts in the play to start with, the virtues like INTEGRITY, HONESTY & FAIRNESS are shot right out the window! Gina came home one day and said, "Dad, they are disgusting." Tommy said, "Sweetheart, your Mom and I always told you to excuse yourself." Gina smiled, "I know Dad. I know. I just go to the bathroom anyhow."

~

So Todd was quickly on his way, feeling that the metal pipe in Tommy's hand was waaayyyy too close, and he had accomplished his mission already. Todd walked away saying to Tommy, "Hey, stop by the store if I can ever help you with any audio / visual stuff." Tommy smiled and said, "I will. Thanks. And I'll leave the pipe in the car." They both laughed a friendly chuckle of relief. For

Tommy, it was the nicest interaction concerning the Cwyane School that he had ever experienced.

It's only an elementary school, It's only an elementary school, It's only an elementary school...

~

The All Cwyane Celebration Day is an annual event where the families of all the Cwyane student body come to Cwyane to see and hear their children, grandchildren, nieces and nephews sing and laugh and put on a little show to make their lives a little bit better. The goal should be to build, in their children, an opportunity to grow and gain self- confidence. HA! Fat chance! That was before Lawrenceville Berry came to Cwyane. It now became the Lawrenceville Berry show. And your children would only get their self-esteem stroked and augmented by the amount of money you donated to L.E. Berry personally!

As the students and families filed into the gym, the changes were stark. A huge banner hung from the stage. It might have read, "WELCOME STUDENTS" or "WELCOME FAMILIES", but that may have been too magnanimous for Master Berry. What it did read was the following: It read, "WELCOME, LAWRENCEVILLE BERRY"! The lights dimmed, and the crowd of families fell into silence.

A single podium stood in the middle of the stage. At previous Celebration Days, the stage was filled with displays made by every grade. Beautiful projects of flowers, or cartoon cutouts or rainbow tri fold boards littered the stage. It made for a child-centered or better a student-centered program. But today, there was only one child. And he made his way to the lectern. Master Berry was about to give his homily.

As the cameras and video recorders began to film, Master Berry rose from the over-stuffed Queen Anne chair on the stage. It was his throne. Everyone else sat on folding chairs. Then, Master Berry hesitated to give his adoring crowd time to focus. He was considerate. Unfortunately for him, no one really cared. Then he began to speak. Along with the photography by grandparents and aunts and uncles, Master Berry hired a professional film crew to video record the event. It was his big day, and at one thousand dollars an hour, he wanted to shine for posterity. A Cwyane parent who was a professional photographer offered Master Berry to film everything at the school for free. Before he could start, this parent at Cwyane was stymied by The Master. L.E. Berry found out that this parent was a Muslim. He was summarily dismissed as to not offend the true blue blooded Americans at Cwyane. "Why he could be a terrorist or a pedophile!" Master Berry promulgated to himself. The parents name was Charles Mountbatten ~ distant relative to the Lord by that name and P.M. Nehru. So much for religious tolerance at Cwyane. Gandhi wept.

Little did any family member realize, they had charged their cameras, phones and recorders to last an hour to film their little ones and any other added attractions that they might want to make a keepsake. But those charges wouldn't last that day. Master Berry was to have his day. And he did. He spoke for two hours. He spoke about his goals for Cwyane. He spoke about his "community". He spoke about the special people at Cwyane who were making his dreams come true. He went on, and on, and on……. The batteries died a slow death.

Before the first song was sung by the pre-kindergarten classes, the cameras went dim, and the kids were unruly. The relatives were confused and upset. But something sadly unreal was happening. In the crowd, a small army of Cwyane parents were nodding up and down as Master Berry pontificated. It was Grandparents Day at Nuremberg. The zealots were mesmerized. They were sponges. They were in the Berry Cult of Personality.

Master Berry spent the last half an hour begging for money. He didn't come right out and plead, he did it by embarrassment. Master Berry proceeded to exclaim about every CD, light fixture and scoreboard bulb bought by a relative of Cwyane child over the year. He asked the purchasers to stand up and be applauded. It was like a bad "Price is Right" show.

As people fidgeted in their seats, uncomfortable relatives didn't know if they should take out their credit cards or checkbooks just so they could leave. Some thought that the communion plate would be passed down each aisle soon. Some thought Master Berry was going to sell raffle tickets soon. It was an abomination of greed.

The most bizarre part was that the Berry Faithful lauded each word of praise from the mouth of the Master. They looked as if they were in hysterics as they cheered his fateful words of acknowledgement after acknowledgement. These people had sublimated their own worthy selves for the adulation and societal status of Master L. E. Berry. He would lead them into the future of education. Like the devil being cast out into a herd of Swine....

It was like a Benny Hinn revival. The only thing missing was the number to call or the credit card machines at the back of the gym. And the zealots had the best seats in the auditorium. The Army of Master Berry sat in the first three rows of seats. The Pre K and 1st graders be damned if they couldn't see over their parents! Mom and Dad poured out money like flowing waters from Bank of America to Master Berry. The parents were there to be noticed in their seats. To immortalize Master Berry on the stage. To augment their position in the Cwyane social registry. It resembled any number of Episcopalian Churches or country clubs. Money buys you a better seat closer to the altar. They think God takes credit.

Some parents of the unwashed got up to leave. If only to go to the bathroom as the program neared two hours plus. But just then, after recommending each person buy at least ten dollars in raffle tickets before they left the building, the pre-k erupted in hilarious laughter. Somebody just pooped their pants. Then the kindergarten roared. Someone pee'd in the aisle. Even the kid who did the defecating was laughing hysterically. That'll save his parents a lot of "shrink" money one day! In fact, the ridiculous set of circumstances made every group of students go bananas. It was a donnybrook!

With no mechanism of control at his disposal, Master Berry raised the volume of his microphone. He spoke…AGAIN! "I have implored all students that the source of all bad behavior is the core of your soul. Right now I am seeing a great deal of **"Black Souls"** out there." Tommy shook his head. The visitors for the day looked at each other in shocked amazement. DID HE REALLY SAY THAT TO OUR KIDS?! The shock of it was quickly extinguished by the zealots of Berrydom sitting in the audience. As one, these people, parents and sycophants rose in their seats and proceeded to stare at their own children of choice. Whether the children were theirs or not, these cultist glared at the children before them. Master Berry glared as well. He spoke, "I would like to commend the helpful friends of Cwyane Community for using the discipline technique that we all learned at the Growing Child Seminar we held this past winter. For their poor and "Black Soul" behavior, I will be cancelling today's performances for the day.

And at that very moment, a beautiful scene unfolded. The large number of visitors roared with sarcastic clapping! One elderly gentleman said, "I thought he would never end." One stately grandmother quipped, "Remind me not to waste my camera's batteries next time."

And just at that moment of the cheering by the visitors, the students nearly trampled each other to see their relatives. They climbed over chairs and rows, and they hugged and kissed them in great joy! Nothing happened on stage or in the auditorium, but the love of family poured forth like a spring! It was something that no school like Cwyane or Master Berry or a donation could buy. It was straight family love ~ void we are prohibited.

The torrent of families with grandkids pulling grandparents by the finger to their classrooms to see their drawings was priceless. They would all soon leave for a trip to the candy store!

~ Ah, but that would be in a perfect world ~

At Cwyane this day and at that very moment, the students just sat there in humiliation. They were broken like mules. Their grandparents looked at their watches. The show ended with what Thoreau wrote about most men, or in this case children, living in a world of quiet desperation…..

~

So how does a Cwyane revival meeting take place? Well, it can happen anywhere at any time. At a sporting event, The "Farm", the supermarket or the hallways of Cwyane can serve as the venue. It is much more than an after school dismissal gaggle outside the gym. It happens every time there are at least 10 Cwyaniacs or consenting parents to participate. But the one thing it must have is Master Lawrenceville Elwood Berry. The straw that stirs the drink. And I mean the Kool Aid flowed.

It started with his presence, unctuous words and his lecherous smile like the Cheshire cat in Alice in Wonderland. Then the Mad Hatter would do a quick two-step into a group of people and begin to speak. "Hellllllloooooooo!" was his normal effeminate introduction. It was a knock off from some A&E show on female empowerment, and it always seemed to stop the group's speaker in a heartbeat. Cwyaniacs in the group would say to themselves, "Oh we have an audience with Master Berry. We are in the "in" club now ~ I hope everyone is watching this."

Master Berry would proceed to giggle, bounce his head, throw his head back in ecstatic bliss, smile broadly, look intently with his hand holding his chin and then hold some part of the people spell bound with an arm on the shoulder, grasp of the elbow while shaking a hand or exhibit the "Berry Hug". It was a sorority house alumni event. Replete with too much makeup and too little character.

I mean he hugged everybody. He hugged and hugged and hugged. He hugged lamp posts, and he hugged trees. In psychoanalytic terms, he was attempting to control people through innocent physical contact. When did your principal attempt to hug everything in his sight when you were at school? Exactly, as a pedophile, your principal would have been run out on a rail.

"The Hug" devoured Cwyane. Before you could say teddy bear, the whole school was hugging everyone all the time for everything. If a student drank a carton of milk at lunch, he got a hug. If a book was returned to the proper library bin, you got a hug. If a cupcake baked exclusively for Master Berry tasted good to him, you got a hug. It was a regular hug fest. Ever try to hug the check-out girl at the store for bagging your groceries? ~ That's right, you can tell it all to the judge, buddy. Tree huggers had nothing on Master Berry's hug-a-thon. "Hug and be dug" for want of a better 70's term. But really it was "Hug for my love" which Master Berry was using to create his adoring cult of misfits, ill-begets and various cougars looking for sex.

During pre-school, hugging each other is a normal play activity. Children are in many ways open to all forms of affection with the hope being that they aren't going to be molested by a stranger. But as children become 4th, 5th and 6th graders, touching becomes awkward because pre-puberty is an awkward time ~ and touching a girl (including Mom) let alone being in the same room with a girl is almost as unsettling as kissing your Dad on the lips. Yikes! But at Cwyane, a troubling development began to occur around the Hug Jamboree and The Helicopters swarming around the place. The hovering began to extend itself across familial lines. The hugs became common among all people, all the time and with all the children of the school. It started to extend to anyone, anytime and it was getting…in the words of Gina Stugats… "a little creepy".

Creepy wasn't the half of it. As these young boys growing into adolescence were dominated by their mothers, hugged by every mother and man at Cwyane, and hugging every girl and boy they could get their hands on, the desire to experiment with just a little bit more sensual wandering or "groping" overtook these boys. And with a very unisex mentality, the boys began to experiment with each other in the locker room. It wasn't only the effeminate or gay boys. The burgeoning hard-nosed, empowered, emasculating young girls were taking on an interest in the physical development of each other in the locker rooms as well. Was it the Hug Fest taken to extreme by Master Berry that was the root of this all? Kinsey might concur. And pedophiles notice it too…..

Before the day began, Master Berry held a school wide assembly. And he lied. What else is new? Due to an outbreak of the flu, Master Berry retorted, "We will be refraining from hand touching and hugging until further notice." Teachers began to cry, effeminate boys began to whimper, brutish girls began to pound their fists into their palms, and the remaining pre-pubescent kids let out a huuuuuggggggeeeeeeeee sigh of relief. "Thank God, no more having to hug that fairy Todd anymore!" one little boy said as he sat in the gym with the rest of the boys lacrosse team.

~

As the students looked on, they could hear sirens. "Sounds like cops!" said one precocious Law & Order tyke. Nevertheless, the burgeoning Detective Munch was right. Police vehicles pulled up to Cwyane. They escorted five people from the grounds. One was a volunteer "Uncle" of one of the Cwyaniacs, another was a volunteer "Cousin" helping out in the kindergarten, another was the "Nephew" of a teacher, and the last two were so distantly related to any Cwyane family that it would take a genealogist to figure out his or her blood line. The pedophiles were led out. The lax security at Cwyane with "volunteers" strolling in and out of the building unescorted and unregistered was as epidemic as large as the Hug Fest-ing. These perverts were in the school because somehow the family or a student's relative gave money to Master Berry surreptitiously and requested the opportunity to teach or to "help out in the classroom." OHHHHH, they helped out in the classroom all right! They made Jerry Sandusky and Penn State look like altar boys ~ hmmmmmm, strike that ~ eunuchs!

Students were kept from seeing exactly who was involved in this travesty as the abusers left the building. Master Berry had arranged for everything to be quiet and serene as the arrests were made with the students and everyone else in the school attending the "Flu Announcement". The only fly in the ointment were the sirens.

Always the megalomaniac, Master Berry telephoned the chief of police in the City of Cwyane to avoid using the sirens upon leaving Cwyane. Chief Brody told him, "I'll put those sirens on full blast if you ever try to pull another one of your "Flu" charades again, you pompous ass!" yelled the Chief! Master Berry cringed as he heard the sirens blare as they left Cwyane. There was a new enemy of his cult. But this guy had "police powers". Master Berry thought confidently, "But I have Divine Powers." And so it goes.

It's only an elementary school. It's only an elementary school. It's only an elementary school…

Then the "Wellness Director" of Cwyane (whatever the Hell that is) began to talk to all the students at the "Flu Assembly" about how proper nutrition can help students escape flu like symptoms and lose weight. This anorexic bulimic "Wellness Director" always concluded her presentations with some form of weight loss program ~ I wonder why? Being convinced that the nationally recognized statistics on childhood obesity were wrong, Miss Wellness decided to lower the weight charts to her OWN specifications accordingly. Talk about justifying your job. So as children ate snickers bars, drank diet coke and indulged in Cheetos from the Cwyane lunch room ~ they were going to be used as lab rats to lose weight and gain it at the same time. Little did anyone know, Master Berry had a percentage of the vending machines in the lunchroom café.

It's only an elementary school. It's only an elementary school. It's only an elementary school…

In order to quell this potentially dangerous pedophilia situation that could ruin both his and Cwyane's reputation, Master Berry devilishly conceived of a retort. It wasn't very complicated. Manson, Koresh and Jim Jones found it successful. Before the day was out, Master Berry put his helicopters out on gossip assignment: to destroy Chief Brody. Blame him for an over-zealous attack on Cwyane because we here at Cwyane know how the town folk feel about our "Special" group / community. It took only 15 minutes. Brody was a goner. The Hueys flew to their cellphones and air ways to broadcast the message of "Hope" that the persecution of Cwyane would end. Social media exploded on this one. But it isn't what you think. Even the parents of the molested children were convinced to understand how seductively provocative a 1st grader could be when they attempt to seduce an adult for candy. It was Heaven's Gate gone viral among the Cwyane faithful. Zealots to the end, the secret would remain amongst the entrusted warriors to protect the Cwyane mystique and reputation. Obviously, Tommy and "The Excluded" were not to be made privy to any of this. Master Berry went room to room in the school imploring students that it would be their "Black Souls" attempting to "Get Out" if they did not bring their troubles and questions: First, to their teachers and then to the "Cwyane Community." ...... Instead of their parents. Next right, Penn State.

But little did Master Berry know, he was going to be done in by the future of technology. As the deluded Cwyaniacs called people on their sell pones, their kids were up to something else. Social media, baby! Before you could say, Joe Paterno Knew, Instagram, Twitter, Facebook and any number of other social media outlets were broadcasting to the world about the "pedophilia problem" at the Cwyane School! No matter how hard he tried to deflect the problem on to Chief Brody, the pedophile consequences fell right into The Master's lap, and he was the focus of blame. You live by the lie; and you die by the lie, and the pen being mightier than the sword! ;)

"There is no need to bother your parents with such matters." Master Berry chastised the students into obedience. His Malignant Narcissism knew no bounds. Lyndon Johnson would have admired his leadership ability, and the "pooh poohing" of the "Nervous Nellies." "Keep it in the community," Master Berry espoused to the little ones. Gina told Tommy about the comments. Tommy vowed to make things right! Gina said, "I tell you everything Dad!" "I know Kid, I know." said Tommy to her with that knowing smile of good parenting well acclaimed. Social Media did carry the day!

~

In a final act of desperation, the Freak Five decided to implement financial warfare on Tommy Stugats. They thought they would start, by not donating money to Cwyane. As I've said before about Cwyane, you need to "Ohio State Buck up" to get your moderately talented child anything like an award or role in the school play. By cutting off the mother's milk of "this" private school, the Freak Five thought they would get Tommy Stugats tossed out for sure. No money; No ticket to Play at Cwyane.

Under the subterfuge of darkness, Lawrenceville Berry met with the Cwyane trustees to conspire as to what might be the best method to remove Tommy Stugats from Cwyane. The Master knew that his Freak Five would carry out his battle plan. So, as Master

Berry packed the Board of Trustees with doctors, soccer moms, workout instructors from LA Fitness andddddddd just about anyone else who had "no clue" about education, his trustees concurred.

Nevertheless, there are certain things called "sunshine laws" that government has to abide by in our country. But the Cwyane Private School 401 (c) 3 (A Non-Profit Corporation) did not believe that they did. But the IRS did……"Sunshine laws" mean that the public must have access to the meeting, notes and minutes of the meetings in order to monitor decisions or actions of the government….and the private schools getting a non-profit tax exemption. Again, those little boring things called "democracy" and "constitutions" that Cwyane did not have to abide by. Cwyane was a feudal state and Lawrence Berry was the Feudal Lord of the Cwyane Estate….seized fee simple in domain…or so he thought.

The initial financial attack on Tommy appeared in a mailing by Lawrenceville Berry to all the people of the Cwyane

"Community". In this expensive portfolio mailing, a graph was published as a centerfold among the many multicultural Cwyane photos in the school's bucolic setting. One poor student was used in almost thirteen photos of the twenty found in the mailing because of his Hispanic-American Ethnicity. It was like a shell game of minorities to claim the high ground for racists. Because the numbers of minority students at Cwyane and the students of color were in the very low single digits, they became the over represented face of Cwyane on every mailing, portfolio and brochure. The parents of these kids would laugh hysterically every time they would see their kids face plastered up on the billboard near their house or the pamphlet espousing the word "DIVERSITY" at the bottom. One of the parents called it "reverse lynching"! He and Tommy laughed uncontrollably! And the madness continued…. But Master Berry kept the "Oriental" or "Asian" student photos to a minimum because as he would say, "You know how they flock with each other and take over a school environment." His racism knew no basement.

On the centerfold of the portfolio, there was an alarming bar graph. It illustrated that while the pre-k and 1st grade parents were donating at nearly a 100% rate, the other grades were merely at a 30% rate and some even lower. Gina's class was at 10%. The Freak Five had mounted a tremendous attack. Lilith knew that her hard work of gossip and underhandedness would yield scornful results and eventually exile for Tommy. She smiled like the Grinch.

Also, as part of the attack, parents under the guise of the Freak Five began to inundate the Trustees and Master Berry with letters and email's explaining that if some grades were not donating that…*something must be done*. So with letters in hand, Master Berry confronted the board in a fraud that they all were complicit. With a record of this fundraising problem, the removal of Tommy would be complete. And if he tried to fight it in court, the record of the meetings and letter would be used to back up the reasons for his dismissal on financial grounds. But little did Lawrenceville Berry or any of the Trustees realize that when you "open the door" to attorneys, all your board minutes pop out like 75 Ben Franklins….

~

Tommy strolled into the store in the Cwyane Shopping Mall with guarded optimism. He wasn't sure if the owner would remember him or his promise to him for help if he needed it. But, he was hopeful that he might remember him pumping gas.

Almost as soon as Tommy entered the audio/visual store, he heard a roar of happiness. "I'm so glad you came in Tommy! How you do'in?" came from the shopkeeper. It was his new friend Todd at the gas station, and Todd said to him, "I didn't think you'd ever come in, but I'm damn glad you did. Forgive me again for that stupid stuff at the mini-mart." Tommy nodded with understanding, and thanked the owner for his friendliness.

"So what can I get you Tommy?" Todd clamored.

"Well, Todd, I need to hear some things…" Tommy spoke with a beguiling grin.

~

The auditorium was filled with parents viewing projects from every grade in the school. The theme was women's issues. It always seemed to be some women related issue many thought. The previous year it was Women and Marriage through the centuries. The year before that it was Women and Families in the America's, and before that Women and the Labor Force, Women and the Wars, Women and the Depression, Women and the Gilded Age….. Tommy couldn't understand the incessant need to topic women every year when a little diversity of subjects might help children expand their learning. It was similar to the reading lists that each grade had every year. It was constant repetition of the same topic.

The reading lists were like a Disney movie. A parent dies and the child gets a harrowing life experience. The school claimed it had no pattern, and each book was a prize winning work. Tommy would soon find out better.

As Tommy walked around the projects he listened. “There he is again.” “Doesn’t he know he isn’t wanted here?!” “He thinks we don’t know what he really is all about ~ a damn WOP mobster.” “He’s a pedophile...did you hear that one?!” The “Lu Lu” was when the statement was made how afraid so many parents are to come to the school because they think Tommy Stugats is going to pull out an AK47 from his London Fog Coat and blow everyone away! The terror was palpable!

Tommy just smiled as he strolled around the projects. Swirls and twirls made a comforting breeze for him as he looked at each project as the gym seemed to warm up on that spring evening. Each child would be in absolute panic when he approached each table!

Their parents WARNED them of him! The parents scurried away ~ leaving their children terrorized and confused in their own minds. The collateral damage of relational bullying is on the bullying kids in the end.

As the evening went on and on, no one was ever sure why Tommy Stugats smiled at them that evening. Most times he stayed with Gina and travelled the room, but tonight he was circling all the projects alone and with great glee it appeared…and it all sounded wonderful to Tommy. Loud and clear. He couldn't believe the malice spoken about him. He smiled at people, and then, they would "shun for fun", and then, they would gossip relentlessly about him. Tommy would turn, and he'd hear EVERYTHING, "I bet he has a gun with him RIGHT NOW! I am going to tell Master Berry!" That one made Tommy laugh out loud a little too loud as eyes near him fixed on him in his mirth. Tommy bit his cheek so hard so as not to burst out in laughter! He said to himself. I should have done this years ago.

The truth was that he was hearing the deep seated malevolence towards him for the first time because he always seemed to get the "twirl" at most events and not the "words". But this time, the little gizmo in his ear that Todd gave him was changing all his perceptions. It fit snuggly. It was small and almost invisible. It could pick up a conversation loud and clear from nearly forty feet away. It was a bug that would make Tricky Dick proud. Tommy was wired for sound, and remotely recording everything for posterity….or court….

~

When Lawrenceville Berry congregated with Trustee members around one of the Women and whatever projects that evening, Tommy heard all he needed. And, as it would turn out, so would the jury. Lawrenceville Berry slyly looked at Tommy and said, "He doesn't have a chance this time. With each class's donations down, it gives us legal recourse to throw him out on the economic grounds that he is hurting the school fundraising by his presence. And, I'm almost definite he has a gun under that trench coat of his…" Tommy kept in range to hear more. Berry went on, "Lilith, Em, Betty and Tammy have been wonderful at agitating and shunning him for me. They constantly tell people of his Mafia background, pedophilia and wife beating even when they aren't true. (Berry chuckled) My, what a wonderful game they are playing for us." Tommy boiled inside his overcoat. He knew in his gut that what they were all doing was all true. Now he heard it first-hand. And back at Todd's shop all of it was being remotely recorded. Tommy calmed himself thinking that Todd and his friends were probably howling with laughter at all they were hearing. They would all pass it along the City of Cwyane's grapevine in a minute. Newton's law was in effect: For every action, there was an opposite and equal reaction.

Tommy walked up to Gina who was playing with her friends and kissed her on the top of her head. "I love you Peanut." He whispered to her. Gina smiled, "I love you too Dad." Tommy left into the suddenly, chilly, spring time night air.

~

As Tommy kept listening, and Todd and the local gentry listened, some amazing tales found their way into the nearby town gossip mill. Tommy and Todd planted bugs and wiretaps on every single phone, cell phone and room at Cwyane. They bypassed the toilets. A little to disgusting… There was one particular story that deeply disturbed the local citizenry. It was a recording of Lawrenceville Berry terrorizing a child with God by his side. To the utter defense of God and The Lord Jesus Christ, Lawrenceville Berry was using them much like his pastor father had done a million times before in his church.

The recording took place one day outside of Gina's classroom. Tommy had come early to Cwyane to pick up Gina and carry her extra projects and sports gear for her. Sometimes Gina could carry almost 30 lbs. of things to his car. Talk about creating back problems at an early age. Nonetheless, as Tommy began to gather Gina's things at her locker immediately outside her classroom, he overheard Lawrenceville Berry address Gina's class. He was speaking in a cadence and in an alliterating manner that had Tommy fearful that a religious sermon had pervaded this secular private school. In a flash, Tommy turned on his ear phone and the tape began to roll in Todd's back office. What Tommy heard and was transcribed onto audio tape and written transcript was not only disturbing but it bordered on a crime. Threatening a child is an illegal act. Of course, brainwashing is legal. And if Hitler could brainwash an entire nation, then Lawrenceville Berry might gain success in brainwashing.....an elementary school class.

~

What was spoken next was bizarre if not frightening. It was R rated, and this was a G audience in Gina's classroom. As Tommy listened, he heard these words come from Lawrenceville Berry's mouth. Headmaster Lawrenceville Berry said this to a group of young elementary school students no more than 9. Master Berry said, "You, as people, need to know that if you do bad things here at Cwyane, it is because you have a Dark Spirit in your heart. You will be judged by our community if you do allow you 'Black Soul' to rue your actions here at Cwyane. And furthermore, you are required by 'our' laws here at Cwyane to bring all problems to people in our 'community' first and foremost and <u>never</u> to your parents. We will be your community family."

Tommy almost fell on the floor. His cell rang instantly. "Did that fucking guy actually say that!" screamed Todd in the phone. At that moment, Lawrenceville Berry opened the classroom door to leave. He had the face of a petrified child when he saw Tommy standing there. Tommy smirked slyly at him, "Seen any Black Souls lately Larry?" Berry announced with great hubris and desperately trying to gain control of all things, "Aren't you supposed to be in a designated area for pickup?" Tommy countered deftly. "Not when I'm helping my daughter carry her bags after your sermon...I mean a class..." Tommy quipped. Berry flinched. He knew Tommy had heard what he said. He took on a look of narcissistic rage, and he quickly shuffled down the hall and out of sight.

~

The attorneys dressed in pin stripe charcoal suits exuded such class that it seemed a shame that they were all whores. The cherry wood that covered the walls seemed to add an air of seriousness to the proceedings as the stenographer took her seat. The room had ten lawyers, a table and two empty chairs. It had style to it, but with every passing moment, it seemed to look more like a cheap Monte Carlo night at a private school. The noise in the hallway clamored with shouts, ridicule and bombast that seemed greatly at odds with the obsequious behavior of all the people gathered into this court house room. Lawrenceville Berry entered the room in his seersucker suit which was, fashionably speaking, a little late in season for this late September day. He sat down in one of the empty chairs nestled between his five lawyers. On the other side from him directly across the mahogany table was another empty chair set between a phalanx of another five lawyers. Then the door opened. In walked a conservatively dressed woman with graying black hair in a small bun. She was the size of a dwarf as she sat down in the last empty chair; thanking the attorney for helping her get seated. She had manners, and surprisingly so did the lawyer ~ at $800.00 an hour, he probably would have shined her shoes too. The stately dressed lady smiled to all in the room. Judge Gertrude Steinowitz looked across the table at Headmaster Lawrenceville Berry III and quickly lost her smile. The she shook her head up and down. It was post time. Immediately, the attorney for Mrs. Eleanor Wellis spoke, "Mr. Berry, exactly what is a Black Soul ~ and could you elaborate your definition for us all as it pertains to the missing $2,500.00 that Mr. Stugats had given to you." THE MADNESS OF LAWYERS SHRIEKING COMMENCED.....!!!!!!!!

Lawrenceville Berry had started to grow very small at this point. He started shrinking into his chair until he almost looked like a crying 2nd grader in the principal's office immediately after some kick balls were reported stolen from the recess room. He just kept getting smaller and smaller and smaller without saying a word. No longer was he sitting in the over-stuffed Queen Anne on the Cwyane Stage. It was more like a folding chair at a funeral home. As the judge restored the room to silence, an attorney interjected, "Well, Master Berry, perhaps you could enlighten us as to the practice of ‘shunning’…we have some audio tapes if it might make it easier for you to remember…” ERUPTION AGAIN! At that moment the room exploded in lawyer screams of objections that sounded more like a hen house with a fox in it than a legal proceeding. Mrs. Wellis bit her cheeks to hold back her laughter and joy from it all. It may have been a hen house of lawyers, but the only fox in the room didn’t have his rooster tail wagging any more. Someone had clipped it off and was wearing it as some sort of virtue pin. It was a very strange place for a fox’s tail or even a feather in one’s cap after all that had happened at Cwyane.

It’s only an elementary school, It’s only an elementary school, It’s only an elementary school…

~

He slammed his hand to the table in utter terror! His body shook with fear as the saliva fell from his mouth as he came out of his short rest on the top of his school house desk. His arms flailed as they came out of their huddled position in anguish. Lawrenceville Elwood Berry III was in chaos! His narcissistic veneer had worn off like scales falling from a shedding snake. He was exposed for the hypocrite that he had always been, and he feared others knowing that he was....a phony. He could see the sun light peeking into his window on that cold November day. The bell had awoken him and his demons again. He had no peace. The rooster crowed without him three times.

He heard children in the hall. Then he wiped his mouth of hanging spit and began to adjust his shirt and suspenders. He wondered how long this torment could last. It was affecting his teaching. He couldn't afford that now.

~

As Mr. Berry wondered to himself as he heard the clock ticking loudly the seconds before 7:57 am. What had happened? It all seemed so perfect. It was all going so well. It was growing into what he had dreamed. His dream was so close. All to be foiled by an "eye-talian" he thought again to himself in despair. His bigotry had no shame. How did it all occur so fast? In a blink of an eye, it was all gone.

Larry Berry stood from his desk, and he re-arranged his chalk. Then he dusted off his erasers and then forlornly descending back into his desk chair exhausted. He had fallen so hard. But why he thought again? He was caught between disbelief and rage. It was like being in the Middle East.

~

The children took their seats at their desks and began to talk. The American Flag waved a bit from the closing of the room door.

Larry Berry looked at it, and he remembered how he once had students recite his pledge of honor and goodness along with the Pledge of Allegiance at Cwyane. His head fell down.

~

Then in a blink of an eye, Mr. Berry spoke, "OK, children. Please get out your workbook to page 11. We will begin our study of nouns, WHERE, WHEN, HOW and sometimes WHY….." With those words, Lawrenceville Elwood Berry III wondered to himself how his life had been transformed from Headmaster of Cwyane into a substitute 2nd grade teacher. It had become a life of nothing more than WHERE, WHEN, HOW and always WHY for him now…. He just stared at the picture of Benjamin Franklin in his room. He spoke to himself in a whisper, "25 of them." Never underestimate the Federal Subpoena Power of 25 Benjamins.

A small voice kept repeating something in his mind all day long, and he just could not free himself of it. It kept repeating. His dreams were scorched with this incessant refrain:

It's only an elementary school, It's only an elementary school; It's only an elementary school…

"For what doth it profit a man, to gain the whole world, and lose his soul?" Mark 8:36

Made in the USA
Charleston, SC
23 April 2014